HORROR COMEDY STORIES OF JOHN OMAR LARNELL ADAMS

JOHN OMAR LARNELL ADAMS

authorHOUSE®

AuthorHouse™
1663 Liberty Drive
Bloomington, IN 47403
www.authorhouse.com
Phone: 1 (800) 839-8640

Published by AuthorHouse 12/11/2019

ISBN: 978-1-7283-3949-8 (sc)
ISBN: 978-1-7283-3948-1 (e)

SPECIAL THANKS TO:

The following Horror Authors: Stephen King, Clive
Barker, RL Stine; Anne Rice, HP Lovecraft, Dean
Koontz and Edgar Allan Poe for writing stories that
made want to check every fear I had and the ones I
would meet later in life. Thank you for inspiring me.

Lastly to my wife Jennifer Broadway-Adams
and all are children and grandchildren.
You all make life worthwhile.

THE WITCH IN OUR VILLAGE OR TOWN

"I was bewitched. No, maybe possessed." "Magic was done to me. Well it was witchcraft." "I had no control of myself whatsoever. I live in Ireland." "Living in the town of Longford is simple with a simple life." The thing is I have lived here my whole life and everyone has their own life or job. Mine is the job of being a blacksmith. Lately I have been hearing rumors of a witch living in our town.

It seems ridiculous to outsiders of Ireland. They have forms of magic, witchcraft and sorcery around the world. I thought lustful, evil or despicable men, teenage girls, adult women; single women, female social groups or old ladies practice magic or witchcraft. There hadn't been a Wicca coven or group of witches in 200 or 300 years in Longford. I know this is the modern age; the thing is people still practice Wicca or Witchcraft. It is where it stands I'm intrigued to investigate this further because the local police don't want to look into this at all for fear of being cursed, going insane or being turned into animals by a witch for trying to cross them. As I walk along this morning around my hometown, I see my Uncle and it is early in the morning around 10am, I checked my watch and that was the time it was today a Sunday October 2nd.

1

I greet my Uncle, by saying "Top of the morning to you Uncle Simon!" My uncle reciprocated this by repeating the usual Irish greeting in the morning as I did, "Top of the morning to you Sean, my wee boy!" We shook hands. He asked, "Where about are you going on this early morning lad?" I then explained to him that I wanted to personally investigate the matter of the rumor of a witch in our town. My Uncle Simon stated and asked of me, "Why would you want to investigate whether or not if there is a witch in our great, lovely and beloved town?"

He adds, "Do you want a spell put on you or die because of your curiosity from rumors of a witch being around us?" To further my position, I told my Uncle, "I just want to see a real witch & convince that said person to leave or move elsewhere that's all Uncle." I continued, "I am not shitting you and I mean that." My Uncle nodded and so I bid to him, "A see you next time," to my uncle and made my way to further my investigation.

As the afternoon crept up on me, I decided to go eat at a pub and maybe "grab a pint" if I maybe want. I was trying to quit drinking. The day was beginning to go forward. As I reached the pub, I was glad to be near it because I felt hungry. As I opened the door to the pub and walked in, I began to be greeted by my server. She said, "Welcome to McCreary's Pub!!" She continued, "My name is Taryn and I will be your server and top of the morning to you!" It was 11:15 am. I answered the same saying to her. Then I asked her, "Where can I sit my lady?!" She led me to it a booth near one of the windows and said, "Right here dear." I sat down as she lain a menu down. She asked, "What would you like to drink?" She added, "There is an unlimited tap of Guinness when you order a pint to go with your meal." "Yes I would like a pint of Guinness dear," I answer her. She tells me to look the menu which I do and then answer her quickly, "Yes I would like your beef with gravy, mashed potatoes and broccoli." She says, "Great choice sir and I will bring back your Guinness." She walks away and tells the bartender to fix me a pint of Guinness. The way you fix a Guinness pint of Stout is you pour the beer tap by pulling it and having the pint glass at a tilt and pour the stout halfway, and stop letting the foam lower in the pint glass and let the stout settle and then pour again until your pint glass is full with foam on top of the pint glass of Guinness.

Once she brought me a pint of Guinness, I sipped and swallowed a wee bit of the stout. Then I set my pint glass down and began to think about how I should go about investigating this rumor of a witch in our town. As I was deep in thought, my food had been prepared and I had a keen thought that my server Taryn had laid my food down, and she asked; "Is there anything on your mind dear man?"

I explained to her about me doing an investigation of the rumor of a witch in our town. She tells me, "You know that's like asking Satan for a favor, don't do it!" Then I nodded in agreement with her statement. I told her, "It's not something I particularly want to do it is just if I can convince her to stop her dark magic practices and just as well convince her to move out of Longford."

Taryn says to me, "That may be an endeavor." She adds, "I know the witch's name it is Jeanette O' Grady." She lastly states, "Maybe you should question the people of Longford and their connection with her and also about her." She adds as well, "By the way here's your food dear man." She laid it down. It was steaming hot! I thanked her as she walked away. With that I began to eat my meal. Also I had wondered how Taryn had known of Jeanette and that she was a witch. Jeanette was a classmate in school. We were dear friends playing about with each other.

As I took my knife and fork, then began to cut the beef with gravy into four equal parts, I sipped my Guinness again and swallowed again. Soon after doing this I began to eat the beef and moved back and forth between the beef, mashed potatoes and broccoli. I chewed pretty slowly and as I did soon began to ponder what questions I could ask people in town about Jeanette and their connection to her and about her witchcraft practice.

As I continued eating this way and drinking my pint of Guinness in that way, I began to notice my pint of Guinness was dwindling away. I motioned for Taryn to come back for another pint of Guinness. I felt a bit of a buzz from the stout. She walks over and asks, "What's up?" She adds, "Would you like another pint of Guinness my dear man?" I answer her, "Yes beautiful I would." Maybe it was the buzz from the Guinness or maybe I couldn't resist the urge to gaze at Taryn she was beautiful with brown hair, pretty thin with a small-medium bust and pretty thin-medium legs and tiny ass. As she walked away, she turned and said, "If you keep staring at me like that we may have to settle down together and start a family too you handsome man you." I blush at that notion. I answer, "You may be right, we may have to marry." After I finished eating my meal, I paid for my meal. Thanked all of them in the pub for the good lunch. I gave Taryn my phone number and she gave me hers. Then I said goodbye and left the pub to go back to my home.

I began the walk back to home to complete a project for my blacksmith work. Walking during this chilly Irish October afternoon, I noticed it was still sunny. I began to smile because of the nice day. As I walked, people were waving because everyone in town knows each other from school or their neighborhood in Longford. As I continued my walk, a little boy threw a rock which hit me in the shoulder.

The boy said, "I got you mister!" I answered the boy, "That you did young wee little boy." He runs away laughing as I laugh too as I walk near my home. After this happening I had reached my home which is 335 Leary Road. I unlocked my front door and see my car in the driveway.

It is a Dodge 300. I always liked American cars so I special bought one with some of my savings from boyhood. I settled in and washed my hands. Then I put my apron on, and begun to sit in my front room chair for a breather. After getting my bearings and my breath, I began to get up and go out back to my workshop in the back of the house. I went through my kitchens backdoor and unlocked it then went through it after opening it and proceeded to go to the workshop.

After reaching the workshop I had to look for the project I planned to do this day for work.

I saw my project a group of horseshoes to be made for some of the horse stables throughout the United Kingdom.

I grabbed a semi thick piece of metal, I then began to
draw with a stencil pencil horseshoe designs in the metal
piece. Put work gloves on. I took a mini laser piece
and soon begun to laser the designs to make complete
horseshoe pieces. As they fell soon after a while there were
thousands of horseshoes made from this piece of metal.
Soon I had gathered the horseshoes and placed them in
the cart to be placed in the back corner of the workshop.

I clapped my hands at a job well done then took off my
apron and hung it on the back wall of my workshop.
I cut the light out in the shop and began to walk out
of there back to my front home. As I got out of the
workshop, and I then afterwards locked it back up.
Made my way back to my home and entered the back
way. I cut the light back on it was pretty dark inside.

The light shone throughout the home and I made my
way to the kitchen, went to the kitchen sink saw the
hand soap and washed my hands with the soap and cut
on the faucet. After washing my hands, I dried them
and began to pull food out of the refrigerator, consisting
of beef, potatoes, broccoli and biscuits. I prepared them
and cooked them in my oven. After they were done, I
put them on a plate and ate most of it, then placed the
leftovers in Saran Wrap and placed it in the fridge for
tomorrow. I decided to get some sleep so I changed into
my night clothes and cut out the lights in the house.
Afterwards went to bed and not before
planning my investigation for tomorrow.

As I began my further investigation, I began to traverse my neighborhood to get more information on Janette O' Grady. I remembered her from elementary school and after 5th grade I heard she moved to another part of town. You would think with most people in Longford knowing one another there would be more information to make this personal investigation even easier and thorough.

The first house I went to were the Jackson's a couple that was near my age. The thing is I figured if they were near my age they knew of Janette's whereabouts and the place she lived. So I went by there and knocked on the door.

A deep but welcoming male voice
asked, "Who the hell is it?"
I answered, "Your neighbor Sean McCreary
who lives down the street has a few questions
about a specific person that's all man."

My neighbor opens the door and says, "Fucking shite, Sean why didn't you say so in the first place buddy!?" This is one of my neighbors Seamus Jackson, he and his wife Julianne live four houses down from me to the right. They are a nice couple and their getting ready to have a set of twin boys. I ask Julianne, "How along are you Julianne dear?" She answers, "Well Sean, aint you a site for sore eyes eh?" She continues, "I am 5 months along now, only four more months and my babies come forth you know."

"Aye, I see now and they will be fine and happy boys God willing it you two, I say to them both. Seamus says to me, "Come on in Sean and have a proper one won't you?"

"Thank you very much Seamus and Julianne,"
I say as I get inside to their home.
After making my way inside, it was a really
nice home with the furnishings and television,
kitchen and well done bathrooms.

I told them, "You have nice digs people." They told
me, "Thank you Sean for the compliment of our
abode." I started by saying, "Now let's get down to
business." The Jackson duo then asked, "What's up?!"

I said to them, "I would like to ask you questions about
Janette O' Grady who may or may not be a witch."
Seamus and Julianne asked me, "Why do you mean to
ask us questions about whoever that person is Sean?"

I told them, "To try and find her, then have her stop the
practice of Wicca and have her move out of Longford."
Julianne asked me, "Has she bewitched
you or something Sean?"
I answered her, "No actually she is an old classmate and
I just don't want her to do something she might regret."
Both of them said to me, "Well we don't know her
and you shouldn't go against a witch Sean." I nodded
in a sad agreement. Told them both thanks for
their time and left their home for other travels.

I went to another house, this time the Morrison's
home another four houses down from me.
They were an older couple in their 60s. The man of the
house and father of 4 and grandfather to 8 is named
David and his wife is Leona. Their house was nice the

only thing is it needed some paint to it because the paint job of before was starting to fade and chip a bit.

As I walked up the sidewalk leading to their home, I made it to the front door of this seemingly comfortable home and knocked on the door. A calm and homely female voice came from behind the door asking, "Oh, who could you be now at this time in the afternoon?"

Then I answered as more polite than possible, "It is me Miss Morrison, Sean McCreary who lives down the street to your left and is your neighbor." She opens the door and says to me, "Good lord, it is you Sean my boy. She adds by asking, "How are you this afternoon dear boy?"

After hearing the hospitality I answered, "I am well Miss Morrison, and the afternoon is bright and sunny eh?" She answers, "Aye, you're right." She says, "Come on in and I will fix you a proper drink."

I do come in and see David Morrison sitting and reading the local paper, and he looks up from it and asks, "Oh Sean, what brings you by on this great Irish day in the fall season?"

I smile and say, "Well I am doing a little investigation into an old classmate who is rumored to being a witch." David and Leona ask me with a look of concern, "Why would you go looking for trouble with a witch and not trying to value your life wee boy?"

Sighing, I say to them, "It's not that I don't value
my life, the things I have heard are rumors if I
can find my old classmate and talk to her about
giving up the dark path and lastly moving out
of town hopefully she can find the light."

Leona says, "That is plausible." She then asks
me, "Who is this witch may I ask?"
My answer hit her kind of hard when I said
her name to her, "It is Janette O'Grady."
David asks, "Wasn't she great friends
with you in Grade School Sean?

I answer him, "She was a great friend, and I just
wonder what could have made her practice Wicca
of all things." I ask them, "Is there anything
else you all know that could help me.

They said to me, "Try the Farrell home in
North Longford for maybe some answers."

I thanked the Morrison couple and walked out
of their home and said goodbye to them and
decided to break out the Dodge 300 to drive
into North Longford to see the Farrell clan.

As I went to yet another house and this time it is now
into another neighborhood now in North Longford.
The house I make it to is the Farrell family home.

As I walk up the walkway of sidewalk to their
front door, I have a high hope of finding

Janette, and reality hits and I might just hear "I never heard of that woman!" I shake my head with the sobering thought of being let down again.

Reaching the front door of the house, I ring the doorbell and hear from behind the door a calm voice a lady of near middle age. Who asks, "Who pray tell is it on this wonderful Irish day?"

I answer her with a calmer voice stating, "It is I Sean McCreary from West Longford and I need a few words with you all." The calm voiced lady says, "Oh okay, if a few words is what you're selling come right in man."

So I am soon led through the front door by a brunette woman at the end of her thirties, with a great body and gorgeous pale face. Her husband sits in the kitchen and reads the local Longford paper. A medium sized man with red hair. Then he introduces himself as Raymond Farrell and says, "Top of the morning to you Sean." He adds by asking, "What would you like to talk about my friend?"

I begin to explain my plight in investigating Janette O' Grady, who is a rumored witch and that I am looking to have her move because a witch in this modern age is bit off putting. His wife begins talking and says to me, "My name is Lynette Farrell and I think her being a witch isn't all that bad when you look at it Sean."

I had thought about it and said to her, "Maybe you're right Lynette, if she were to bewitch me it rightly might serve me right." I added, "Then my assumptions would be served right." Raymond answers, "It is no need to put your life or even sanity on the line to fulfill a notion of a witch in our town."

Then I asked them, "Do you any of you know Janette?" They both answered, "Why no, we moved here from Dublin and are getting settled in as we speak dear Sean." I then said to them, "It's okay, at least I have your confidence in me with some apprehension." Both of this two person family said to me, "We wish you well in your investigation of this witch and god speed and safe travels and when you get back to her and be safe Sean!"

I waved goodbye to them and began on my way out of their home got into my Dodge 300 and made my way back across town. As soon the moment when I arrived back home, I had decided to call Taryn from the pub to go for a date with her. I missed her.

I called the waitress from the pub named Taryn. There were a couple of rings on the other end. After three rings I heard her familiar voice. It said, "Hello this is Taryn." I told her in an answer back, "This is Sean McCreary, and I am sorry for not getting back to you sooner honey." She laughed a bit with confidence and said, "It's alright dear man, you called and I couldn't be happier." She adds, "What's up Sean baby?" The courage I mustered was palpable as I said to her, "I was wondering that if you're not too busy in the next two nights to going out to dinner with me gorgeous lady?"

She answered me, "Since you show confidence
and are a handsome man, I will go out
to dinner with you a definite yes!"
I stomped a bit at the good fortune and luck I had
received and said, "That is great Taryn!" I add, "You
are off in the next two days I take it dear heart?

She answers with a laugh, "Yes dear man I am."
"What time will you pick me up honey?" She adds.
I told her, "I will pick you up at 7pm my dear."
She says, "Well it's a date dear man."
I asked her where she lived and she told me, "400 South
Longford Avenue in South Longford." I thanked her.

With that I said, "Goodbye and thank you dear Taryn."
She told me, "Goodbye and your welcome dear man."
We hung up the phone simultaneously. I decided to go
back over to my work in the workhouse out back.

After setting up a date with the waitress named
Taryn, I had begun to start work on more horseshoes
for horse stables throughout the United Kingdom.
After finishing the work I went to sleep and two
days later the fateful day of our date was upon us.

I drove to South Longford to pick her up at her
home. She wore a dark blue dress. Had her hair let
down and she was even more beautiful than before
I had seen her with her hair tied up in the pub.
After she got into my car, I asked her "How are you
this evening my dear and good evening too!?"
She answered, "I am great tonight now
that I see you handsome man!"
She kissed me on the cheek and I smiled as the car was
put in reverse to get out of her driveway to drive out
and go near the restaurant we were to eat at this night.

We drove to North Longford where the restaurant was and
we had then arrived at Good Old Shenanigans restaurant.
I parked in the parking lot and we both got out of my car.
I had begun to drape my coat around her shoulders
because it was a chilly October night.

She said to me, "Thank you dear man." She
added, "You are a fine gentleman."
As soon as we reached the front door of the
restaurant, I opened the door and let her go in first.
Then she said, "Thank you very much for opening
the door for me Sean you handsome man!"

We made our way to the beginning of the restaurant, a hostess greeted us she had red hair and blue eyes. She had a nice shape to her just like Taryn. She asked, "How many in your party?" We answered, "Only two people here." The hostess said, "Good I will take you to your seating area." She led us to the seating area and gave us menus. She told us, "My name is Sarah and I will be your server." She then walked off. Taryn had begun to ask me a question asking, "So Sean what is that you do for a living may I ask?"

I answered her, "I am a Blacksmith, gorgeous lady." She chuckled at that notion, we had discussed many things that night, including about our childhoods, our parents, family members and school life. After our food reached us, Taryn began to stroke my leg intimately, and said to me, "After we finish how about we go to your place and have a proper fucking Sean dear man."

Me being the man I am smiled and said, "Let's finish this meal and hit my pad and do some proper fucking!" After eating our meal, we kissed after leaving the restaurant and made our way to my car. I unlocked it and she got in before I did and then it was started and we then drove off.

After making our way to the house, we were making out and made our way to my bedroom, she slipped off her dress, bra and panties. I took my clothes and things off as well. I made my way to her snatch and licked then poked it with my fingers. She moaned. I then slipped my dick into her and we started to properly fuck which went through the night and we went to sleep after climaxing.

After sleeping with her, I had awoken the next day
with her in my bed sleeping next to me. I leaned
over and kissed her gently and softly, she had
awoken to me kissing me her and she slipped me
the tongue. It was great and I felt rock hard again.
Then we proper fucked each other again before
showering and eating breakfast in my kitchen.

She had me cook for her and I had to show her
that my skills were not just in the bedroom.
After making her sausage, eggs, toast and bacon with
milk. She sat down and ate it slowly and surely. When
she was through chewing and asked me, "So Sean how
has the investigation about the witch been going?

I answered with the first frown I have ever showed
her, "Well Taryn, my dear lady it has been rather
shitty really." I added, "Barely anyone gives me any
good information except you." "Thank you for all
your help so far baby!" I lastly stated. She answers, "It
was nothing dear man, you seemed determined and
I thought that helping you out is the least I can do
for a well thought out gentleman such as yourself."

"By the way did you know where Janette
O' Grady's parents live?" She states.
Then I answered, "No do you Taryn dear?"
After hearing that she stated, "Yes, I do they live
on 700 Longford Drive in Southeast Longford."

I told her, "You sure know a lot about Janette, Taryn." She answered, "When it comes to Wicca rumors you hear about them often enough Sean." Thinking for a second, I state, "Maybe I should come from out of this home of mine and get to know everyone as I should."

Taryn giggled and said, "You're right you should get to know more people in Longford." We both laughed and finished our breakfast and then showered and had sex in the shower too. After giving her some of my clothes to wear back home, I took her and dropped her back at her place in South Longford and waved goodbye to her as I walked her to her door. Then I got back in my car and drove off.

I thought out loud as I drove off back home to prepare for tomorrow, "So I have to drive to Southeast Longford to re-meet the O'Grady's tomorrow?" I added, "Fuck me sideways!"

I ventured to another house in town.
This time it was Janette's parents
home the O'Grady's house.
When I walked up to their home, I saw a face peer
through the window and then close the blinds. I guess one
of them heard my footsteps creeping toward the house.
As I made my way to the front door it opened
and an older lady with brown hair came to greet
me and said, "Oh dear Sean my wee boy come
in it has been a long time." I answered, "Yes Mrs.
O'Grady it has been long time hasn't it?"

She then said to me, "Come right in Sean dear man."
So I walked in a man waved at me then said, "Sean,
who could be son in law have a seat." So I went in
and had a seat in their living room." Mrs. O' Grady
had begun to tell me in a kind voice, "A little bird
told us that you were looking into Janette being a
witch." She then asked, "Is that true dear Sean?"

I answered her in as calm of a manner I could, "Yes
Mrs. O' Grady it is very true madam." Mr. O' Grady,
well Melvin and his wife Bernadette O' Grady said
to me, "So Sean you don't remember the ritual that
Janette and….. Mrs. O' Grady kicked his foot and he
stopped with his saying. I had begun to feel a wave
flow over me as he mentioned the ritual. A flashback
came into my mind, there was Janette and another
teenage girl, her face was being hidden by blackness.

Mrs. O' Grady rose up and asked, "Are you alright
dear boy?" I put my hand to my head and said

to them, "Yes I am fine, it is just right when he
mentioned the ritual my body felt a wave flash over
me and my mind began to remember something."

Mrs. O' Grady said to me, "Good you remember
then." I answered her yes madam." She began to
talk in a manner that was familiar to me and said,
"Her name is Janette Sharon O' Grady. She grew up
in this house." She continued, "You went to grade
school together and in high school she performed
a ritual on you. She was also your girlfriend."

Then another wave formed on me, I remembered
in another flashback bugs and darkness ran
over me. Janette tried to come over to me.

Her mother then said, "She comes from a
long line of witches, me included. How do
you think I got Mr. O'Grady wee boy."

Mr. O' Grady said to me, "She lives in NW
Longford on 1000 Mill Road." He continued,
"You will find all your answers there dear boy."
I told them, "Thank you Mr. and Mrs. O'Grady." I
continued, "I will now leave you and ask her everything."

With that I left their house, waved goodbye
to them, unlocked my door; put my keys
in the ignition and drove home.

After learning the witch's full name and location
in town, the day would soon come when I
would have to reface Janette again. I had hoped
to see her under a different circumstance.
As I had begun to drive over to my house to think of a
way to do this interview with her and not be hurt at all.

Then I saw a notepad on my kitchen table, it had
some writing on it. Which said, "Use this to plan your
course of action when facing Janette," signed Taryn.

After seeing this, I felt a rush of relief that she cared
enough and seemed as if her love knew no bounds.
I thought to myself that I must thank her personally
when I see that hot and sexy face of hers again.

I began to write a plan when I reached Janette's home,
I wrote get myself inside, ask her direct questions, and
convince her to leave Longford gently and calmly.

All this excitement made me feel better. I felt that
doing this made me feel like a real detective. So I
decided to make myself a meal, which was some
turkey from America and chicken with broccoli,
cheese on the broccoli, rice and a roll with a Pepsi.

After eating this meal, I felt better. Thoughts of
Taryn flowed through my head as I walked toward
my bedroom. Just some of her scent flowed through
my nostrils as I made my way through the hallway
leading to my room. As I made my way into my

room the remnants of the sex escapade from my
time with Taryn hit me in a rush of smell.

I thought to myself out loud, "God damn!!!" So I
went and grabbed an air freshener can and sprayed
a little bit in the air." It mixed with smell of sex and
was something I would now have to deal with.

I smiled and said, "I did this with her." I had
begun to change into my sleep wear.
After wards I went to sleep.

The next day after completing most of my work
for the day, I got into my car and drove off
toward Janette's home in NW Longford.
It was now night and I made it to her home.

I ventured to the witch's home on the
end of town where she lived on.
I walked up the walkway to her home and it was a
very nice and homely home from the look of it.
I couldn't rightly believe that Janette could be a
witch with such a great looking home. Hopefully
the information I received from the O'Grady's and
Taryn were false and that Janette was just a regular
citizen of Longford and not a witch at all.

As I begun my ascent up the walkway, I heard
creepy sounds that were normally normal except
on this night it was terrifying. I had heard a wolf
howling in the background where the forest was.
Then after that bugs were chirping and making
other insect like noises, it made me very uneasy.

I was having a creeping fear wash over me.
Just then I heard a screech, I turned to look to
my left and then to my right. Low and behold
it was grey cat making the scary noise.
I went to go near the cat as I came
closer to it, it started to meow.

I started to stroke the cat's fur. It purred
and meowed even more.
After a while it stopped and began to talk to
me in an Irish accent of a human voice asking,
"You must be Sean McCreary aren't you?
Shocked I backed away thinking the cat was
evil. It laughed and said, "Don't be scared

dear child the fun is just beginning." It walked
off slowly then ran away laughing.

I said aloud, "If that isn't the weirdest shit I ever
seen and heard, by god I know I'm not crazy. I
added, "That fucking pussy spoke to me."

I walked closer to the front door and saw it had a
doorbell. So I rung it and waited for her to come
to the door and I saw her lights were on as well.

After I rung her doorbell, I heard her somewhat
familiar voice which was different then what it
was like when we were children and teenagers. She
asked, "Who is it on this wonderful evening?"
I answered her, "Dear Janette, it's me your
former boyfriend Sean McCreary and I wanted
to speak with you about something is all."

She opened the door and I was awe struck by her beauty.

Her red hair, pale skin and dark blue eyes were
intoxicating. I seemed that I would barely get the
words I wanted to say to her and try getting answers.
So I started by asking her, "So Janette, I hear
you are a witch is that true dear woman?"

She answered me, "Yes dear Sean, I am a witch." She adds,
"The rumors are true my love." She then lastly states, "I
have a regular job, I work at a tech company in Dublin."
Hearing this I didn't feel at ease, yet I felt
better knowing the rumors were true.

I then asked her, "Why would you still be a witch
even though you work for a tech company?" She
answered me, "Well just because I partly comply
with modern preconceptions doesn't mean I
can just leave my real life behind baby."
So I feel somewhat cheated that after starting
this conversation and she won't leave her life
as a witch behind so I ask her, "Why don't you
quit and also can't you leave Longford and live
elsewhere with your witchcraft practices?"

Sighing, she says, "To believe that you would
come to me without a lot of baggage Sean, it
seems we have to do this again eh dear heart?"

I asked her, "What do you mean by we
have to do this again Janette?"
I hear the front door of her house open and close
again. I try to turn around and see who it is,
Janette raises her left hand and I can't move. Some
darkness comes from her and moves toward me.

While standing in her living room, the darkness crept up on me, and also it seemed insects had begun crawling quickly up my leg. As the insects began further crawling, I begin to have creeping fear wash over me again as the bugs were beginning to crawl up my other leg and falling from the ceiling and onto my arms, shoulders and head. Some were even on my neck.

The darkness went by onto my feet it then began to cover my feet, shins and the rest of my legs. The insects began to cover my entire body now. As the darkness begun to cover the rest of my body, I had felt coldness coming over my body. Then I felt numb now.

As the insects and darkness began to mix together on my body, I felt a similar panic and terror just like that flashback I had at the O' Grady's home. As the darkness began covering my face and entering my mouth, I had let a scream to my horror no sound came out. The darkness was everywhere now.

After the darkness subsided, something strange happened.
I had begun to see my life in windows as
I was in a dark abyss of darkness.
Pieces of my childhood had begun to be shown to me
such as walking for the first time, eating ice cream, etc.

My preteen and teenage years came next my life with
Janette becoming even that more clear to me. I had
seen us making out after school. Even us engaging
in sex knowing it was our first time with anyone.

There was always some one around us a brunette,
she seemed familiar. The only thing is every time her
name is called the name of this girl is censored.

The next memory is the three of us in the woods
and Janette takes me by the hand along with the
young brunette girl. Janette stops with me hand in
hand at a specific spot in the woods. She begins to
ask me would I marry her. I answer her yes. Then
she begins to say some Wicca incantations. The
young brunette says some Wicca incantations and the
same darkness that came from Janette in the living
room comes to and covers me in the same manner
in her home. Bugs begin to fall on me as well.

I feel the same horror and terror I felt in her living room,
I begin to start screaming and my voice is muffled just
like before. After it engulfs me the memory stops. I
begin to see a memory of myself in my twenties and
being an apprentice to a blacksmith learning the trade
as well getting knowledge and wisdom of life too.

I then see myself getting my drivers license and going into business for myself as a blacksmith. The next memory is of me buying my home. After that some time goes by and I see myself from a few days ago, meeting my Uncle and going to the pub and meeting Taryn. The other days show up in my memories as well the investigation of Janette. Asking people about her, then finally off going over to her parents' home, going to her house and the same questions I just asked her. The darkness and bugs enveloping me whoever that person coming through the door and being I haven't met them yet.

The darkness was stopping and was slowly fading away.

Once the bugs, darkness and other animals dissipated from me I began to feel I couldn't move. I began to come back to reality. Janette was giving me a blowjob and stroking my dick at the same time. I saw another persons head licking my asshole. I saw that it was Taryn and I said to her, "What the fuck Taryn are you doing?" She answered, "My parents told you there was another person who was with you two during the ritual wasn't there?" The thought had finally come back to me just like before bugs and darkness had crept onto me just like the ritual from when we were teenagers. Taryn had begun to say, "The reason I didn't reveal my name was to not trigger your memories from before." She adds, "Didn't it seem strange to you seeing me again and while working at a pub?"

She lastly stated, "How could you not remember that Janette and I are sisters?"

I nodded and felt the pleasure of the blowjob Janette was giving me. Janette stopped and said, "We set this up to have you stay with the two of us and be betrothed to the two of us." I felt too good to answer and instead had begun to feel like I would orgasm as Janette went back to giving me a blowjob. Taryn had begun to lick my asshole again while fingering my asshole as well. She asked between licking and fingering my asshole, "If we didn't let you come to us would you have tried to find us honey? I had felt too good from these actions happening to me and I said, "Oh shit!" I had come inside Janette's mouth who had then kept some sort of chalice near my balls. She let some of my semen come out of her mouth into the chalice and jerked my dick to get the rest of my man milk out. After releasing my essence into the chalice, I fell backwards even more to the floor. I had hit my head.

Taryn and Janette said some Wicca words over the chalice and a white smoke came from the chalice. They stopped and took turns drinking from the chalice until I heard them both slurped out the rest separately. The two of them trembled and shook. A white aura appeared around the two of them. They took off their clothes and were stark naked.

They went to me on the floor and stripped off my clothes, socks and underwear. They both separately and together engaged in sex with me. They told me we were having sex magic. I was still in a bit of a daze from the blowjob and the orgasm. I smiled from the ecstasy of this happening which was the sex magic that is.

I orgasm med in Janette first and then Taryn begun to work my dick to and then I orgasm med in her too, just then after coming I had felt spent having an orgasm so many times in a row.

Janette told me now still naked, "Sean my love, we will be married won't we?"
I answered her, "Yes my love we will eternally be together now and no more looking into you being a witch ever."

Taryn said to me, "You know you're mine too don't you dear man?" After this romp, I put my

clothes on and left Janette's home and drove
back to my place to reconcile my thoughts.

After the ordeal, I felt like I had been
used by the two witches.

It seems my life got better after getting back with Janette
and now with her and Taryn's love, I could be happy and
content with life and not be a bachelor forever. Some
days I feel a recollection and remember the following:

"Now that my life changed from these events currently,
I remember The Witch in Our Village & Town."

<u>The End</u>

WHERE IS THE PURE EVIL?

In a Salt Lake City, Utah suburb a group of people ranging from teens to elderly people searched the Salt Lake City area for evil. They would go about their day, going to school, working or staying in a retirement home. "My name is Johnson Five a silly name for a native person of the Americas as a person that I am." Due to White America assimilating my people into White American culture my family was given an Anglo Saxon surname. My native name is Wolf Howling at the Moon. I am telling this tale because Kosata still mingle over and live on our entire homeland of what they call the Americas. May they be black, white, brown or creamy colored or tan skinned they don't belong here. Also I am forced to call these Kosata "my fellow Americans." "Even though the country of America is and always will be a joke by starting as a country that is broke and in debt it remains still broke and in debt". "The story of shitty America and the other nations, well the other shitty nations of the so called "Americas" is for another day."

It seems those searching for evil in Salt Lake City, found it and they are being carted off to prison or juvenile detention for their mischief, chaos and mayhem. Watching them from afar I noticed they were all trouble. I smile now knowing these evil Kosata can rot away their natural lives in juvenile detention, then prison or are already going to prison.

As any other day in Salt Lake City, it would be warm, hot, cold or chilly. On this day in May, I walked with my girlfriend Janie Silver. She's another Native Person of the Americas like I am. Her native name is Watching Owl. We casually walked around town looking to pick somewhere for us to have a date on a certain day. I asked her in a smooth voice, "So Janie, where is it you would like to eat on Friday night?" Today was the last day of school. Well we were in high school as we were in 10th grade. We skipped school today. We start 10th grade in August. She answered with a tone of voice, "How about the diner near the city bus depot!" I answered her, "Sure we can go there baby." We had known each other since we were children, at first we lived on the Shoshone reservation outside of Salt Lake.

Our parents grew idle and disillusioned with life on the reservation life it is good and bad. Good because it is where we are our own people, culture, history; art, food, music; and language. Bad as in we don't get much help from the local, state or the federal government. Some people have lived below the normal standards or some manage and live despite goodness or hardships. After we moved to the city, life changed while living in Salt Lake and we all had culture shock by the Mormons and other Kosata living here.

I was particularly discouraged by the people in the school, some were bigoted and racist against Native peoples from what they seen in Westerns and period films set in the old west and pioneer movies.

As we were walking through downtown Salt
Lake City, we were nearing the city bus depot.
Janie was starting to ask, "So what are we going
to get for food once we arrive at the diner?"
I answer her, "Whatever you like my dear, it's on
me today so let's get filled up today with food and
soda." I then ask her and then kiss her on the lips
after asking, "Is that alright my baby?" After kissing
me back she says, "Let's do that sweetie pie!"

We begin to hold hands and walk closer to the diner near
the city bus depot. Smiling and laughing at the notion
of such a great day to unfold we notice a group of people
either near our age or even older with young adults,
adults, middle aged people; and the elderly converging
near the diner. We both remembered these people were
rival groups at one time and would argue with each
others separate group at any given time. We both asked
each other with a slight whisper, "What the fuck are
these Kosata planning?" So we put our plans to eat at
the diner on hold to see what will develop with these
crazy Kosata going around Salt Lake City's downtown.

The large group of people of former enemies had begun
to say something in agreement that went like this, "We
are going to see where the pure evil is in Salt Lake City!"
The then all say in unison, "Hell fucking yeah!"

The two of us look at each other and say at the same
time, "This can't be good." Just as we finished talking
I noticed my little cousin Rain Fire known to everyone
else in America as John Omar Larnell Adams. I ask him,

he was a little boy at this time or preteen, "What are you doing here Rain?" He answered me, "Just enjoying my vacation here in Salt Lake, your parents told me where you would be." Rain Fire has Cherokee, Blackfoot, Apache, Navajo; Shawnee, Pawnee, Inuit and all other Native Tribes throughout the Americas ancestry.

He looked dumbfounded at the group of people ahead of us and asked us, "What in the world is up with these kosez ahead of us?"

I explained to him where we know the people of this large group of people from and what they are planning and lastly of us watching to see where this adventure of these nutcases will lead too. He tells us, "I will tag along to see this trouble in the making." Janie and I tell him, "Cool we have a tag along buddy for this endeavor."

After watching these former enemies band
together in search of evil in Salt Lake,
Janie and I with Rain are still in disbelief
these one time enemies have gathered together
to start trouble, chaos and mischief.

As we overheard their plan to fuck with
people, destroy property, ruin people who work
lives, and steal vehicles to joy ride in.
We stood a fair distance from them and taking
in the chaos and soon to be mischief.

The three of us had sighed out a sad sigh of trouble
getting ready to brew over into the downtown area. We
had decided to bring binoculars to see if these horrible
human beings doing their misdeeds from afar if need be.

I had wondered as I talked with Janie and keeping
a close eye on Rain so he wouldn't be taken to start
doing bad things with these foolish people.
I asked him, "Rain Fire, you won't join in when
these people do bad things will you?"
He answered, "No Wolf, I won't join them." He
continued, "Even if I did I would try to leave them
behind there is too many people involved with
this and they are "hot" if you catch my drift."

I couldn't disagree with Rain that they were going to call
all kinds of attention to themselves. The thing is Janie,
Rain and me were drawn to this like people seeing a fatal
car crash on the highway. Sure you don't want to look
the fact of seeing death and carnage or even mayhem

tickles the primitive side of human beings who may nor may not delight in other people's misery or untimely demise which predated their death or trouble with the law and you want to see how the aftermath turns out.

This is the reason the three of us want to see this play out because deep down in us, we would cause mayhem, mischief and chaos had we put it in our heads to do these kinds of horrible things to others and to the city we live in or vacation at.

We continued following this band of people
searching for and committed to doing evil.
It seemed too good and close for comfort to these
sick and twisted people plotting evil deeds.
The group of old men were tasked with leading the
group, the old women were in charge of keeping
everything together, the middle aged people were to
organize the different groups to act out their deeds of
evil, the adults were to hand out supplies for evil; the
young adults and teenagers were to act out the majority
of the evil deeds and the other groups follow suit.

We saw there was a method to the group of peoples'
madness. Also we could see they planned this
whole undertaking ahead of today. The thing is
that we wondered where in the hell these Kosata
had thought and worked how all involved could
do what and complete their wrongdoing.

It started to impress us how twisted and malicious
this band of mischief bandits had begun to act out
their fantasy of as a group's evil, and horrible acts.
One of the elderly men said out loud,
"Let's make this bad fun happen!"
The other people in unison said back to
him, "Yeah you're fucking right!"

They had begun to split up and go in all
directions while we kept our distance.
Just like that now, "the shit begins to hit the fan".

Their fun and evil began quicker
than I had seen it happening.
They all walked down the street, we follow a great
distance behind them and only could keep our
eyes on them to see all this crazy shit play out.
We saw the teenagers and young adults stick fruit
into the muffler holes of cars parked in the street.

The adults and middle aged people began to
electronic jammers on the bottom of vehicles. The
elderly began to piss on the sidewalk as they walked,
pulling down their diapers to piss everywhere.
They were even picking their noses and wiping
boogers on everything that any of them touched.

It seemed to us, like what else could these
troublemakers do next. The three of us looked at
each other and shook our heads in disbelief from
this act of evil and chaos in Salt Lake City.
Only time would tell how this would end. We all could
see how this would end, it's just we wanted to see this
problem play itself out and view the resolution.

After seeing the initial trial of this beginning
"wrong kind of party", we kept our distance
and continued to watch this travesty.

As Janie, Rain and I continued from a far distance
from those people searching for and committing
evil, way after they all took a piss on a wall and
pulled their pants up and continued walking down
the street to cause more trouble and chaos.

They saw a couple kissing each other passionately, the
group pulled each of the people as the couple's pants
off and spanked them hard on the ass and pinched
their bottoms. As the couple was taken aback from this
as their pants were by each of their ankles, the group
yelled out at them, "Get a room you fucking perverts!"

Disturbed by the disturbance and having their
pants pulled down and spanked then pinched say,
"You all are assholes for this you fuckers!"
The group walks off laughing. The couple pulls up
their pants and runs off saying, "Those assholes!"
We felt bad for the couple; afterwards we saw their
embarrassed faces as they passed the three of us.

Then we still kept a safe distance from these Kosata,
to keep from getting caught in their mayhem
and becoming victims of the group's "fun".

They continued until they saw a lifeless body of a
person ahead, they smiled in the delight of what
to do next in their quest for chaos and evil.

A man was dead on the sidewalk or so I thought.
So one of the teenage girls said to the others in
this big group, "You know something I think I
will give him mouth to dick." Janie, Rain and I
were shocked at this new development the only
thing is we could not look away as we were curious
to see what these baddies would do next.

The teenage girl walked up to the supposed dead man,
crouched on her knees and unzipped the so called dead
man's pants, pulled out his dong and began to suck him
off with her mouth. She could see he wouldn't wake so
after doing this to him and the young lady decided to fuck
this man to "bring him back" from the dead. The girl
then slipped her pants down, she mounted the corpse. She
inserted him into her snatch and began to ride him like a
drunk girl on a mechanical bull at some country western
bar like my dad took me to when we were lost on the
highway and I saw all those drunk white people in there.

She started to moan a little bit, it seemed this
action was starting to awaken "the dead man".
He started groaning and saying, "God damn
honey your cookie has gotten real tight baby."
The girl started going faster and faster, the
man who was lying on the sidewalk had begun
to slowly be awake. He opens his eyes to the
teenage girl fucking him and says real loud,
"Oh shit girl!!" He continues and gets up after
pulling himself out of her hot box, then says, "Young
lady are you trying to get me put in jail as some sex

offender?" "Shit girl, are you crazy or something?"
He puts his member back into his pants and zips it
back up. Then he goes off in another direction.

The group laughs and points at the guy
walking away and call him, "You homo!"
We look at them in disbelief and watch them continue
on their way up the street to more mischief.

The middle aged people pull out a duffle bag full
of spray cans and begin to hand them all out to
everyone in the group to spray paint walls with graffiti
and make them their own "piece of property".

This group of chaos starters began
to spray paint many walls.
They took some spray cans that one of them had
in a large coat with what seemed to be hundreds
of pockets. He handed all the male and female
figures in the group spray cans to spray with.

They begin to shake the spray cans to make the paint
easier to spray, as the elderly begin to spray paint on
the walls the following words: "Lick my sagging balls
cunts!" The old men seemed not really creative and
really offensive. Another group of words on the wall
is: "Suck my drooping old titties assholes!" The old
women may not be creative as the old men are not
just as well and are just as offensive and gross.

The middle aged men spray painted: "Lick my
bald spot skanks!" See just as stupid as the old
men. The middle aged women wrote: "Lick
my menopausal pussy dickheads!" The great
wonders of a middle aged woman's mind.

The adult males wrote, "Lick my sweaty balls sluts!"
"What woman would really want these disgusting
bastards' balls in their mouth?" Janie asked me and Rain.
We answered her as direct saying, "Hopefully no
woman will want any of these degenerates."

The adult woman wrote: "Lick my asshole and
ass cheeks you pigs!" Rain looked down and
shook his head then sighed and lastly said, "There
really is no hope for these clown ass bitches!"

45

The young adult males wrote: "Suck my
dick, real fast and deep bitch!!"
I am sure their mothers would appreciate
the notion of their sons call and response
to females near the young men's age.
The young adult women wrote: "Lick my cunt
and suck on my pussy lips you ape!"
These women's fathers must love that all their
hard work raising this individual into a classy
woman has gone out the window of decency.

The teenage boys wrote: "Suck my dick, lick my
balls and take my nut in your mouth floozies!"
Janie said to me about this statement put on the wall in
front Rain as well stating, "It is something this pencil dick
making a demand that won't come through eh boys!!!?"
We laughed at her statement.

The teenage girls went last with this parting gift to
anyone walking and seeing this message written as
follows: "Fuck me deep in my ass and snatch and
pound the shit out of both holes and make me come
then shoot your man milk in my mouth dirty boy!"
The irony of these girls that one of them took
advantage of an older gentleman and now they want
even more dick in them, such sluts they are.

The group walked up the street, got materials out
to burn abandoned buildings which they started
fires to and dance as the fires spread around.

After setting fires to buildings, the group quickly ran
away from the blazing buildings and continued more of
their troubling behavior. We followed behind them in
the casual fashion we had done since the beginning.

They began to hoot and holler, "Did
you see that fire burn dude?"
I figured what else could these despicable
people do else to downtown.
I had overheard along with Rain and Janie that
the group were going to start planning to rob some
stores throughout Salt Lake City's downtown.

We watched them get out baseball bats, pipes, bricks and
crow bars to open up the store doors or break windows.

They all went first to a clothing store and we saw
one of the young teenage girls hurl a brick through
the front window of the clothing store. The sound
of breaking glass almost startled us. We saw glass
break and go in every direction. They quickly began
to file in and begin to stuff separate backpacks full
of men's and women's clothes and accessories.

What was left in the store was disposable and worthless so
they decided to set fire throughout the remains of the store
which was almost nothing left inside the clothing store.
The fire began slowly engulfing everything in site and
inside the store, leftover clothes, shoes, hats; watches,
sunglasses, socks and underwear were ablaze.
Rain, Janie and I watched in horror as somebody's life
work was just turned to cinder and a burning lot.

John Omar Larnell Adams

The group walked away and said to one another, "Did you see that shit burn?" They added, "It went Foosh!"

They went around to other stores such as sneaker stores, boot stores, coat stores; etc.

The group began to rob and loot many different stores.
The girls had makeup as did the young adult,
adult, middle aged and elderly women as well in
their jacket pockets. The men had lighters and
cigarettes and cigars for everyone to smoke.

The teenage boys had weed to smoke and the whole
group began to toke on the "crazy bush". As they were
getting high some of them laughed evilly and deviantly.
Some of them complained of heart pain, mainly
the middle aged and elderly people.

Rain looked appalled by this disturbing disregard of
behavior by this supposed civilized group of people who
differ in their gender, age, and height; lastly skin color.
I tapped Rain on the shoulder and asked
him, "Little cousin are you alright?"
He answered, "I am alright its just troubling seeing
others do what I would be doing and now I see what
I have been doing over the years to others and their
property was very wrong from these assholes doing it."

As we made our way through downtown, the
group had begun to go further up the street
and they then noticed a coffee house.

They saw a coffee house and began to go
inside then they locked the front door.
We stood across the street and looked with binoculars
at what may transpire next in this night of mischief.
The group had not notice this and I said it
because there was a vent leading out toward the
street from the front of the coffee house.

So we can now hear everything going
on inside the coffee house.
As they entered the coffee house, one of the female
employees of the place asked the group as they made
their way in was, "Hi and welcome to our coffee house."
She adds, "How can we serve you all today?" After she
said that one of the group and old woman locks the
front door of the coffee house and says, "Oh you can
help us by you and the other patrons of this joint giving
up your bodies to us. Everyone else in the coffee house,
including all the men and women say, "Huh what?"

The group quickly descends onto the patrons
and the employees of the coffee house, and
they forcibly kiss the patrons and the employees
passionately and begin to fondle them.
The people, that the group are fondling asks,
"Why are you doing this?" In between the
French kissing and groping, the group tells
them, "Shut up and enjoy this shit!"

The group begins to take off their clothes as does the
patrons and employees of the coffee house. The orgy
then begins, and the older women kiss and take the

young males in between their legs and fuck them all while goosing them. Goosing is when a male kisses a female or when a female kisses a male and simultaneously sticks their finger in their asshole and begins poking or moving that said finger in their partners' ass to arouse and satisfy them in a perverse sexual manner.

The old men and adult male, middle aged men, young adult men and teenage boys take the female patrons and start sucking on their breasts and begin to double penetrate these women by having one of them get in their hot box and in the back where their nether region is and fucking them to pleasure.

The adult women, middle aged women, young adult women and teenage girls do the same thing as the elderly women, kissing, fucking and goosing the men to pleasure. Janie, Rain and I hear all the moaning and the smell of sex permeates the air as this goes on for 2 and half hours.

After the group climaxes either inside or on top of the patrons and employees of the coffee house, they gather their clothes and put them on and say thank you to everyone at the coffee house and take their leave. The employees of the coffee house along with the patrons say, "Thank you too we guess."

Business goes back to usual at the coffee house and the group unlocks the door and walks out to find some other crazy things to do.

After having their orgy in the coffee house
they all left to cause more mayhem.
We still kept a safe distance from them all to not arouse
suspicion or any violent action from these people.

The group walks a bit up the street as we follow
from our distance away. They begin to plot
out their next deal of trouble to get into.

One of the teenage boys says to the rest of their
group, "Let's steal some rides to crash since they
aren't our vehicles to begin with." The others in
the group say out loud, "Fuck yeah!" Then add
to their statement, "Let's do that shit right!!"

They begin to look around for parked vehicles as they
begin searching with their mischievous eyes they soon find
the majority of vehicles to steal for joy riding and crashing.

One of the middle aged women asks, "Who has the
mechanisms to open these rides for us all?" One of the
young adults pulls a bag with various things and gadgets
and begins to hand them to everyone in the group.

The group then began to freely unlock with apparatuses, cars to steal and joy ride in them around downtown Salt Lake. Some stole Mercedes Benz's, others Ford's, Dodge's, Chevrolets; Buick's, Mazda's, Nissan's, KIAs; GMC's, and other kinds of automobiles and SUV's. To me & Janie's surprise, they all seemed too damn happy to be behind the wheel of cars. They put them in reverse or drove them off initially.

As they drove these vehicles some are speeding up and down the road as cars and trucks with SUV's swerve out of the way and crashing into brick walls of buildings. Some of the group says, "Fuck yeah man!" They continue, "You see that dumb ass crash into the wall?"

As the group continues driving through downtown, some of the take the vehicles and crash through store fronts and into brick walls. They sort of limp out of the vehicle and high five. After high fiving each other and saying, "You're fucking a right dude!" Also they add, "Did you see me crash this piece of shit?"

The rest of the group crashes their vehicles which they stole and begin to plot out their next move of mayhem to commit.

After wrecking and totaling the cars they stole,
they all exited the vehicles and walked to cause
more chaos. These really are evil people. It seemed
nothing except the law could shut down this party.

They decided to let out the rest of the oil and
gasoline left in the vehicles which they had stolen.

One of the elderly men asks to the group, "How about
we set fire to all these piece of shit vehicles eh? The rest
of the group says in unison, "You're god damn right we
should old timer!" After using lighters and paper from a
news paper they found inside one of the vehicles they set
fire to the vehicles and then the cars exploded one by one.

The group was very close to the water company
and decided to plan on going to it. So they
decided on going there to have even more
heinous fun. Such an evil group they were.

They decided to go the water company building and disrupt the system providing water services to everyone in Salt Lake. We seen them go inside and could only imagine what terrible things could go down inside the building.

As they went inside, we saw the security desk inside the lobby and saw where the cameras throughout the water company were filming. The groups had dispersed into different groups and were hell bent on tearing up the equipment running water to most of the homes throughout Salt Lake City.

We saw them from our watching spot away from the water company building and saw each of us through binoculars what they had been doing. While seeing through the binoculars we saw that each of the groups had dispersed into the mechanical room housing the equipment needed to maintain the water flowing in the city. They started tearing up the equipment and spraying water from water guns onto the equipment ruining it. They had all begun laughing at the chaos and mayhem which they were causing here at the Water Company.

After getting out of the water company building they all had begun to leave the building and laughing outside the place. Some of them asked, "Was that shit fun or what people?" The rest of the group smiled a bunch of devious smiles and nodded in agreement.

They then planned since the fact of this matter was their group was near the electric company.

So after thinking about it one of them in the group had said to the group, "Let's all go to the electric company and really have some fun!"

They all said, "Yeah let's do it good people!" They walked in the direction of the water company.

After doing this they went to the electric company and
were going to cause a blackout throughout the city.
After making into the area of the electric company
building, they unlocked the door with a jammer
and lock opening mechanism to get in.
Once inside they used flash lights to guide
themselves inside, once in there they dispersed
into different groups again and went to tangle
up or disturb the power throughout the city.

After they reached the main room, we saw this
because of the security desk in the lobby of the electric
company. We saw them through binoculars going
in that main room and twisting off controls to the
power supplied to everyone in Salt Lake. They began
shooting their water guns at the main machine.

As sparks begun to fly from the machines, the lights
in the machine room were fading in and out. The
group had started to leave out of the main machine
room only to get out of the water company's building.
As all the lights went out, the group laughed hard at
the full on blackout throughout Salt Lake City.

They took their flashlights and continued walking
as we heard police sirens in the background. We
followed way behind to keep our distance and see
what else the evil doers would end up doing next.

The group kept walking as we saw from behind us
people from the water company and electric companies
went to both buildings to quickly put everything back

online as usual again. As the lights came back on and some fountains' water came back on to make them rework again, we followed still in back of the baddies committing mayhem and chaos in the name of evil.

After employees from the water company and electric
company put everything back online. The group
broke into a gun shop to take guns out to shoot
at places and peoples cars to hit people hopefully
if they were foolish enough to be in their cars.
After getting into the gun shops, they put ammo
and the many handguns, shotguns and leftover
assault rifles in their backpacks and duffel bags.

We saw them see a group of people sitting in their own
cars, and one of the teenage girls said to the people inside
of their cars a quick statement, "Heads up People!"
The group took the safeties off of the guns and
cocked them and opened fire, before they opened fire
the people in the cars hit the floors of their cars.

The bullets began going into the cars of these
people some of them screamed in terror. Holes
filled their car doors up. After the gunfire subsided,
the group dropped their weapons and ran off.

We followed after them, as we did the people in
their cars raised up and said, "Those fuckers were
crazy as shit and let's call the cops on them!"

They continued the gunfire into more cars
throughout Salt Lake's downtown. People were left
traumatized. Some were shaking hard. As they kept
going further, we stayed a safe distance behind them
watching their every move to see this play out.

One of the elderly women said out loud, "Let's go get something to eat because I am starved!!" The group went to find a restaurant or diner to eat so they settled on Denny's.

After causing terror through downtown, they decided
to go get something to eat at Denny's. Once inside
they took up different booths. We came inside and
sat at the counter and acted like we didn't notice
them so as they would not recognize us from
following them throughout the day and night.

So Janie, me and Rain had begun to talk a little
in the Shoshone language as we then switched to
English to order our food. We ordered Burgers
and fries with Pepsis. The group all ordered
the Grand Slam breakfast meals each.

After 15 to 20 minutes our food came out, as did the
groups' food. As we ate I asked Rain as did Janie about
what he planned to do while in Salt Lake City. He told me
visit my house, and the reservations and all Native Peoples
in the area because he had not been back in a while.

While we kept talking, the group had discussed
their plans, dreams and aspirations for after
this chaos and mayhem for evil ends.
Some of the old people said, they wanted to live out
their last days in a retirement home or facility and be
visited by their relatives. The middle aged people said
they wanted to be as great elderly people as the old folks
they were doing this trouble making had become.
The adults hoped to be as together as the middle aged
people who were leading this group and be better than
the middle aged people before them ever could be.

The young adults had hoped to be as "on point" as full on adults as say their slightly older counterparts. The teenagers were glad to finally hang out with the "older heads" and try to be as greater than they are whenever all of them reach their elder peoples' respective ages.

This continued until after they finished their meals. Rain said to us, "Let's leave here soon." Janie and I nodded as we tried to not pay attention to the bad group of people getting ready for more trouble.

After they all paid their food bills they left. We stayed and finished our meals. After they went way up the street we paid our check and followed them again. As we followed after them, the group was walking and thinking of a bunch of ways to get away with the chaos, mischief, mayhem and evil they had all caused this night.

As we continued after them still, we all said to each other, "The cops are going to get all these jackasses. As we finished our statements sure enough we saw straight ahead a policeman talking to someone so we stopped and let things work out on their own.

We saw them walk and the cops were talking to a witness to some of their mischief. After seeing them get past two blocks, the witness recognized them and told the cop. The cop got on his radio and notified other Salt Lake cops.

The group nervous began to fall back a little bit and felt confident that they all would get away scot-free. These people were wrong and out of their league. Now all the bad shit they did was coming back "to bite them" in the ass.

We saw the look of terror and fright come over all their horrid faces. They had begun to hear the footsteps of retribution coming toward them. Thumping and getting louder as the footsteps got closer to them all.

Soon they turned and saw what they feared most come in their direction.

The group saw cops starting to get close to
them. They bunched together to formulate
where to meet and they scattered fast.
Once they scattered and ran away, it seemed the
elderly ones and middle aged ones had more pep in
the step than I imagined. They had ran very fast
as did the adults, young adults and teenagers.

While running some of them passed us and didn't
even give us a glance. They were in great fear as the
hands of justice was starting to get ready to grab them
all up and judge them to a severe punishment for
not only breaking the rules and also the law itself.

After running for some time they all met up. They were together again with cops not too far behind. After getting together, out of breath and panting as if the gears of time were slowing for them, they seemed less scared and more dedicated to finding a way out of Salt Lake City to avoid jail, prison and juvenile hall time.

It seemed the footsteps were coming back and the evil doers were starting to feel the icy grip of fear again. The feeling left them reeling as terror and maybe karma was being redirected back at them to give them the trouble which they caused.

The footsteps got closer again, panic waved over them. One of the teenage boys and one of the teenage girls said to the rest of their group, "We have got to get away from the ham salad heads come on people!"

As the police were starting to begin catching up to them, they all used shortcuts to evade the cops further. Soon they were willfully running through all the shortcuts and seemed that getting away was eminent, and all seemed to be going in their favor. That's the thing with criminals who try to run from the law, some stay hidden until they die and others get scared, slip up and get caught or just give up and surrender.

The police were waiting for some of the group at the beginning or end of the shortcuts they used to try getting away.

As the members caught said, "Oh shit man I am fucked for real!" As these individuals said this they were caught handcuffed and lead away by the police officers, who were still going on in their hopes of catching the other baddies running about downtown Salt Lake.

The police as they were in pursuit of the remaining members of the group doing bad shit. They received even more complaints concerning the large group causing chaos, mischief, evil and mayhem.

So other officers were dispatched to find these other mischievous characters still running through downtown, and the cops were looking to use the same tactic hiding in the shortcuts of the area to catch and outsmart the jackasses foolish enough to think they could do all this and not get caught in the end.

Soon not too long after, the cops caught the ones they planned to cut off before anymore trouble could continue from the dumbasses.

The police had then caught up to the rest of
the group and begun to arrest them.

We saw with delight as the group was lead in different
paddy wagons to jail or juvenile hall. That concludes
this story, Janie and me are still together. Rain Fire
is the one who wrote this story as we told him the
beginning. He hopes you enjoyed it. By the way
check what I told him to write at the bottom.

We looked around our metro area and saw then
and still ask ourselves Where Is the Pure Evil?
It was right in front of us the whole time.

The End

A DEMON IN OUR MIST

Once there was something odd that happened in a suburban neighborhood, our neighborhood. It made me wonder if demons or a demon being was amongst us, I will tell you this tale which has good and bad feelings in it.

Where can I begin this story, "Let's see, that it was a wonderful beautiful spring day in March, the sun was shining bright and the flowers and other foliage were growing so green and colorful, and lastly they were all beginning to be in full bloom for the spring season."
My friends and I were enjoying the day as most teenagers in high school do.
We had decide to try and enjoy all the great weather and hopefully find dates for the rest of the school schedule and have girlfriends for the summer.

The day went on as a normal.
We had overheard that some of the people
begun to say that a demon or some evil entity
had begun to appear in our town.
It seemed strange to us, like a big breasted woman
streaking naked at a college only to slip in dog shit and
fall then break her arm only to have part of the bones
in the arm sticking out through the skin to her horror
and some Goth kids and Emo kids laugh at her.

Not funny to you? You don't appreciate dark humor. Well
to be sure not the entire endearing story is dark; some of
it is gross in nature. It may even be truly even macabre.
Don't think I am a sucker who gets his kicks from
telling demon or other kind of horror stories to
people just so they can piss their pants, shit on
themselves or throw up on themselves or others.
No, I am just a guy reminiscing over my past years
from when I was a teenage boy with my friends.

This rumor we had heard made us very curious as
to who or what, when or why there was a demon
or evil entity within or around us in our town.
The town we live in State House in Colorado.

It's a quaint town near Aurora and Colorado Springs,
and a bit away from Denver. We may not be as
famous as the other cities and towns in Colorado,
its just we live quite happy and serene in our
surroundings and are our proud of where we live.

We had questioned each other, and then we
had sought to question others in town.
The four of us decided to go around town and
ask people about this rumor of a demon or evil
being directly among us or out in the open.

We traveled around the north part of town
and stopped at the retirement home there
called State House Retirement Home.
We voted on seeing are grandparents who stayed in
the home. As we went in we saw these elderly people
who we watched at the place were trying to regain the
days of their youth to amusing detail and reverence.

A lot of them were trying to get into each others
pants and some were succeeding. They played
pranks on the nurses, orderlies, chaplain, secretaries,
janitors and activity supervisors and workers.

Our grandparents approached us and we said, "Hey
there Grannies and Grandpas," to each of them.
They answered back, "What's up grandsons!"
We went over by the television and we had begun to ask
them about if they had heard any rumors on a demon, or
evil being or supernatural being in our town as of late.

They answered, "We haven't heard anything
like from the gossiping nurses or janitors or any
of the other silly dipshits who work here."

We laugh at our grandparents no filter in what they say
as you may be accustomed to the elderly talking in this

manner, like children have no filter and say whatever comes to their mind about or on people they meet or see.

Our grandparents bid us adieu as we begin to get up to leave the retirement home. We tell them, "Try not to get into too much mischief and mayhem." They answer, "We will try grandsons." Adding on, "We can't guarantee that shit though!"

Then we begin to laugh and go on our way out of the retirement home and to go interview more people on the rumor of the demon in our town.

The search for the rumored demon
amongst us continued onward.
We searched in the eastern part of town going
through some neighborhoods until we had reached
a house with people we remembered from when we
were Boy Scouts. Just like that we decided to ask
them some questions as to if they knew anything
plausible about the demon among us in town.

We asked the Thomas family about if they heard anything
on the demon in town they replied, "We know that maybe
the demon could be in the foothills or so we have heard."
Just like that we asked them, "Is it really true that
the demon is in the foothills of the city?"
The Thomas clan answered, "We don't know for
sure, it's just the main rumor going around some have
spotted someone doing occult like stuff there."
They add, "Go to the foothills and check it out, because
middle schoolers like you should do one last adventure
before getting into high school and really come of age."

After hearing the news we wanted to hear, and
then the group of us nodded and said to each other,
"Guys let's do it and find this demon, hopefully
if he's bad maybe we can talk him down." The
other guys say, "Hell yeah let's do it fellows!"

We wave at the Thomas family and say goodbye
to them. They wave back and say, "Good luck
fellows and if you have to fight the demon use
dark magic if you kids know any of it."

So we went to go in sight of the foothills outside of town.

I gazed up at the sun on this warm,
sunny and bright spring day.
It warmed so suddenly then quickly enveloped my
body. It felt so good to me. My friend a young black
boy named Thelonious Marcus asked me, "Do you
think we will ever find this demon Steven man?"

I answered him, "Sure T.M. we will definitely find
this demon and all that should be done is us walking
toward the foothills until we find this evil being."
He then asks me, "Do you think we might be
automatically killed or this demon might let us go
to live out our days until we die as old men?"

Just then I reassure him by saying, "Hopefully we will
live and just have a bunch of good stories for our kids
and grandkids to tell when the time is right buddy."
He smiles and says to me, "Let's hope so great buddy."

We both pat each other on the back to slightly comfort
each other on this troubling subject of us meeting the
demon and hopefully staying alive from this meeting.

So the two of us and our other two friends continue
the trek to the foothills outside of town.

It seemed we may have a lead on our demon search.
The Thomas family had told us earlier that this
demon was holed up or even seen in the foothills
outside of town going near the highway.

We all continued to walk in the direction as to where the
foothills were. It seemed so far away, yet oddly close.
The sun had become a bit more intense, even for
the spring the day was slated for 75 degrees.
We sweated a little bit, and luckily one of us brought
a backpack full of water bottles. They were 1 liter
Deer Park bottles. We were slated to have a drink
when the heat began to become too much.
We had took them out handed them to each other, opened
them and had taken a few sips of them. Then we put the
tops back on them and put them back into Cola's back
pack. Later we kept up our pace toward the foothills still.

As we searched to the spots where some people spotted the demon we looked for some trail, which would lead us to the demon. We walked for what seemed that it would go on forever, like the walking sidewalk in an airport except hopelessly never fucking ending. My friend a young Jewish boy Cola Brett said out loud and directly at the air itself, "Shit man!" "Does this trail ever fucking end this is starting to turn into a whole lot of bullshit!"

Our other friend, a young boy of British descent like me named Grant Minister said to him "Don't worry Cola dude it will go in our favor once the trail ends and we find the demon." We had continued up some more and we had finally hit the entrance of the foothills. Cola, Grant and Thelonious had said out loud, "Holy Hell!" They added, "Look Steven, there's someone here." I had looked and noticed the guy up ahead as we continued up the foothill.

We saw a man eating the carcasses of a dead
dog and a cat which was lying on the road.
We began to ask him questions while the two
animals' blood dripped from his mouth.
The main question we had begun to ask him
was, "Excuse me sir, do you know if the demon
everyone is talking about is here or not mister?"

He had ignored us and continued to eat the dead dog
and dead cat. He acted as if he were an ignorant asshole.

We asked him again, "Excuse us sir, do you know
if there is a demon hanging around these parts?"
The guy then closed his eyes and reopened them. He
began to sigh and said in a low register, "Fucking human
mortals and their spawn asking stupid ass questions."
We had begun to realize this man
wasn't what he seemed to be.

After coming to the realization that this
strange road kill eating crazy man might
truly be the demon we were looking for.
So we at last ask him finally, "Sir might you be
the demon we have been searching for?"
He stopped eating the road kill and dropped the
carcasses on the ground. He quickly rose up from
where he was sitting and then suddenly........

The man who was eating the road kill ran off. We chased
after him until he tripped over his own feet; fell on his
face hard with a boom! He pulled up then pushed himself
up only to reveal his nose was bleeding and broken.
He began to laugh really loud and very evil like,
we were kind of appalled at the site of this bloody
nosed and crazy, twisted and nearly evil man.

He had said to us, "You lowly mortals
want to know if I am the so called demon
you seek eh human children filth?"
We were taken aback from this crazed man
saying something so demeaning and just
plain wrong about us that he said.

Then we all said, "You crazy middle aged bastard!"
We all charged at him, Cola quickly took off his backpack
with the water in it and went toward the back of the
crazy middle aged man, Thelonious went to the right,
as Grant went left. While I went to the front, after
taking our spots, we bum rushed the guy punching
and kicking the guy until he went off his feet. We had
begun to stomp the guy as well. Trying to release all
this anger and we felt there was no need to talk it over
with this crazy man or demon so we beat on him.

After beating the man up a little he laughed. We
got up off of him and he had a wave of power or an
aura flying off and surrounding him. He got up,
and then stood on his feet dead center and he threw
us many yards away with his force or power.

After landing we noticed the backpack had flown a bit too.
He laughed some more and asked, "Is that all
the fight you all have in you lowly mortals?"
Still in pain we figured we could beat the
demon with brute force. We were wrong.
The aura surrounding this evil being got stronger as the
air it seemed to melt from the force of his aura and power.
We had some creeping fear wash over
us as we saw and looked dumbfounded
thinking this might be the end of us.

Soon after he flew away, we realized we
were dealing with supernatural forces.
We decided to get back at this demon and do
all we can to win in our next fight with this
demon. That is what we were sure of.
Soon we picked ourselves up along with Cola's backpack
and made our way back home to State House our town.

We told our parents what happened, they
patched us up from our wounds dealing with
the supernaturally powered up man.
Our parents each said to us separately, "Why
would you challenge and beat up slightly a demon
only to get thrown back hard to the ground?"
We all answered as calmly as we could saying
top our parents, "We thought we could win in a
fight, he proved brute strength is just superficial
in a fight, so we need a new strategy."

After spending a couple of days healing, we came to the
conclusion we could try out the dark magic, which all
of the Thomas clan was talking about. So we decided
to gather what little money we had to learn more on
these dark magic and dark arts to battle the demon.

We decided to go over to an occult bookstore
for further research and study.
We went into downtown and found a sort of book store
that dealt with occult matters and we wanted to learn
as much of these dark magic and arts as we could.
We first looked at different books on Wicca, Voodoo,
Santeria; and Onmyodo and Tao magic as we could.

After spending days and time with our
money we had saved up. We became adept
in occult practices and their ways too.
We had begun practicing with each other spells, guards
and object protection. After some consideration we
began to setup some strategies to deal with the demon.
Soon later on more of the same......

We had begun practicing even more what we learned from
the occult books until it all became second nature to us.
After becoming more adept at the dark magic and white
magic practices we had started running partner drills
to enhance each others magic prowess and specialties.
Each time we had begun to become more in sync
with each other and complimenting the strengths
developed and enhanced them and slowly we were
getting rid of our weaknesses one by one.

After getting more practice with the occult practices
and spells and other magic, we formed a plan to
deal with this supernatural force or demon.
Two of us would run point while the others would
be backup for the ones in front or from behind
and deal out more offense and the two in front
could deal with other defenses and vice versa.

We began looking for this being we found before
and way after we had started walking back on the
trail back to the foothills outside of town. Some
of us were going as we planned, while the others
searched and surveyed the area near the foothills
and would whistle whenever we found the fiend.

So then we continued the search for the demon as if we
really had looked to finish our battle with each other
desperately. Our anger was building as we looked around.
Only time would tell if we were to find the
villain of our pent up anger towards him.

We searched and looked high and low until we found the spot we saw in the hills and woods where he was eating the road kill. We saw him sitting in the spot we found him before. He had a devious smile on his face and said to us out loud with glee, "So humans I hope to fight you again." He added by asking, "I look forward to seeing who will win this time, don't you children do too?"

We said in unison, "We will see who can win this fight demon!" As we said that he moved at a blinding speed which we chalked it up to him not being human. He dashed in front of me and Grant he hit us with his fists as painful it was we were lifted off our feet. He waved his hand with seemed like telekinesis and moved us away from Cola and Thelonious. As we flew backwards, Cola and Thelonious sprung into action using homemade Shikigami and Wicca spells. As the Shikigami formed spirit animals to attack the demon he had a look of worry on his face. Cola's Wiccan spell was cast on the demon which binded his body as to which he couldn't move.

Thelonious used the spirit animals to attack the demon, one of them a fox scratched the demon's shoulder. The demon let out a yell and said, "I will shit on you once this is done you little human bastards!" With that the demon began charging up his aura and started to break free of the binding spell and sent Cola and Thelonious flying along with the Shikigami.

Grant and I had got back to our feet and the demon raised his aura higher and began making blades of the wind to shoot at me and Grant. As we saw the blades

of wind forming we nodded at each other. He shot
the blades of wind at both of us. Somehow by luck we
dodged them. Grant began a Voodoo chant to cause
disruption in the whole being of the demon. Some what
his aura was distorted, so I chanted some Wiccan spell
of making a mix of fire, lightening and a wave of water
to hit him at the same time. This was a two way of a
combination, which had hit the demon and as he was fried
by the lightening and charred a bit from the fire. The
water wave carried him a bit down from the foothills.

He turned into his demon form because of the
pain he felt his voice rippled and distorted the
air around us and we were thrown near Cola and
Thelonious. In the pain we all felt coming from
this battle something came about from it.

After doing battle with the demon we felt it was a losing battle. So we retreated and decided to formulate a better strategy to defeat him once and for all. With all things considered we had dealt him some damage. So while we were feeling pain from being hit and getting thrown, we all smiled that we could possibly defeat the demon.

As we left our battlefield, his chilling words left us more determined to beat him severely, "Get stronger and we may have a better battle humans!" We grew angrier with hearing those harsh words. After we made it to our homes we decided later to meet at Thelonious' house to make some sort of plan to get the demon and defeat him.

After remembering his words as we left the demon, "Get stronger and we may have a better battle you weak humans!" We became more motivated and willing to defeat this demon and restore our peaceful days again. We put our fists to one another's and said these words, "We will defeat this evil demon and bring our lives back to what they were!"

We worked even harder honing our skills in the occult
to combat and defeat the demon once and for all.
After rereading the Occult books and Onmyodo books
as well, we had decided to learn all the things contained
in the book. We learned binding spells, elemental
spells, curses, protection and even sealing magic.

We then went over scenarios where all of us
faced the demon and ways to unbalance him
or even cause severe wounds to him.
This running of simulations made us feel like generals
during a war or something. We came to realize no
matter what human they face on or during the war is
small fry compared to our enemy we had to face.

The feeling we got from facing the demon and going back
and forth made us feel alive, just like when we were really
small going through an elderly persons yard knocking
their stuff over and having them chase after us to give
every one of us an ass whipping for being mischievous.
Then getting away, the rush from it all was intoxicating.

My look on face after we discussed our plan of action
said it all for us. My friends gave a similar look of
anticipation mixed with joy and excitement. As we were
trying to calm down we let out a loud cry of, "Ha!!!!!!!"

The fateful day for our final battle came.
We arrived to the foothills with a look so serious it
stirred up feelings of ecstasy to the demon. He said,
"I hope you boys have enough mettle to satisfy my
hunger for battle." He added, "This may be our final
confrontation, let's end our struggle shall we children?"

He entered his demon form from the start, Grant and
I switched back and forth from front to behind with
Cola and Thelonious alternating attacks and giving
room for defense to each of our partners in this battle.
The demon began shooting blades of wind and fire
combined with the blades of wind, which were causing
epic destruction of the landscape of the foothills.

We used protection magic to protect
ourselves from the demon's assault.
We began using lightening attacks, rain and waves
of water, with fire and mini earthquakes to disrupt
and attack the demon. Cola and Thelonious
used binding magic to hold him steady and
used Shikigami with power or aura disruption
magic to stall the demon's aura and power.

The demon began to strain a little to get back at
us. To break free of the binding spell he unleashed
inner aura arms to break up the spell. He took more
damage from the Shikigami again. He began to say,
"You humans have got a lot stronger, looks like I may
have to go full power against you mortals then!"

As he said this his muscles grew more defined, and
he began to move even faster than before. After
seeing this before our eyes got more in tune to his
movements and we had barely seen him get to us.
He broke through our defense and we shot at him what
the stuff he fired at us blades of wind which cut his chest.

His aura arms grabbed and threw us in all
directions, as we landed we went through
with the rest of our strategy against him.
With both causing damage to one another and the
landscape it seemed the battle could go either way
from what we saw and the demon had seen.

After going back and forth with our battle,
we were beginning to hit a stalemate between
us and the demon's demonic force.
We decided to not back down and going to push
forward and find a true strength we only dreamed of
or saw in cartoons or movies we grew up watching.
The demon had begun to over exert him self very much
so. He was panting hard also breathing very heavily.
Our group began to feel the effects of the battle too.
Our bodies were beginning to get
weary and nearly broken.
We had one group of final moves and
spells to put the demon away.

We had sprung into action going in
separately, attacking from all sides.
Cola, Grant and I would be a distraction. While
Thelonious would use speed magic to catch the
demon off guard and plant a seal spell to hell
sending the demon back to where he came from.

As our plan sprung to action, the demon tried to
attack us all at once due to his fatigue he could barely
attack us with his aura arms and blades of wind
with fire. After Thelonious touched the demon with
the sealing spell he said, "The task it's done fellows.
The spell put a very strong binding spell on the
demon and we stood on each side of the demon.

Then we said some magical words and the demon said, "No, you rotten and filthy human brats I lost!" The pits of hell opened up and after saying our magical words he was transported into hell very fast all the while he cursed us all as he descended into the fiery pits of hell.

After defeating the demon and sealing or confining him to Hell. We shouted together in unison at our victory.

"Yeah we won and defeated the demon!" We
fell backward and breathed out very hard
and we smiled at a job well done.
We were even more elated that we won finally. Our
town was now safe from a demon in our lives.
After a while we picked ourselves up and made our way
back into to town. We came with plenty of scrapes, cuts
and bruises on our bodies. Afterwards, we made our ways
to our homes. By the way my name is Steven Center and I
am telling you this thrilling and creepy and funny story.

Once we all healed from the wounds from our battle with the demon in the hospital, we decided to keep everything we saw learned or did a secret with ourselves to hide from everyone in town.

After living through that hell, I realized life is good or troubling with a Demon in Our Mist.

The End

A DAY IN THE LIFE OF DEATH

"Some people on Earth and throughout the universes fear me. It's as if my presence was something they dreaded the most. Let me explain who I am, my name is as most have called me the Grim Reaper, Death God or simply Death. Some have said I lead them on the Dance Macabre where I lead the dead souls on a dance to their graves and later to the afterlife." "Are these things true?" "Yes, I do lead you to the afterlife." The thing is I want to explain is how my day goes everyday. Just your typical day in my life told to you. I was walking around earth, speed walking at a speed faster than any human or animal or vehicle or plane can go. Only a few can see me. When they do, I point at them and laugh to tease them of their impending death. You may ask yourself, "Why does Death use black humor when describing himself sending mortals to the afterlife?"

"Well it's simple really. I just like making my job fun to myself. When you have to lead idiots such as you mortals or gods to the afterlife it gets tedious and boring. Well the good side is my friend known to you all as a martial artist, author, actor; voice actor, music producer, Sometime DJ; music artist/musician, artist, comic book artist, sometime Japanese manga artist and

writer or ghost writer and comedian John Omar Larnell
Adams. He is known to me as his real name Jasay."
He has decided to hang out with me to see my job on
Earth. "So I will begin to explain how my job goes each
day. Join me as I tell you what it's like to be death."

I glanced at the large vehicle collision or accident, wondering "Do I have my work cut out for me today?" So I took my time to analyze this horrific human catastrophe. I saw a woman impaled by her steering column. The look on her face as she was killed really was to die for. She had looked very terrified.

I saw her spirit standing with a hole where her heart used to be. I imitated sardonically her terrified look on that shameful face to her and she was frowning at me. The bitch can't take a joke.

The semi truck driver who caused the massive pile up of death and carnage was looking at his body inside the truck with his crushed body. He seemed distraught. So again I sardonically imitated him with his hands up saying "No, please not now!" Just like as he did and he was not amused. This is yet another asshole, which who really doesn't see the dark humor in their deaths which they cause the dipshits.

The terror on his face showed his death his death was quick and painless or slow and painful. His tractor trailer separated from the truck hitting the other 10 or 20 cars. It had been killing the other 45 to 50 people. I saw them as spirits too. They were spooked seeing Jasay and me.

They asked, "Why now death?" Jasay now as his young boy self shook his head in their stupidity. I told them to follow me. I also told Jasay to wait for me as I lead souls to where they went in the afterlife. Then after talking with Jasay, I had begun to the dead folks to heaven, hell, limbo; and purgatory. Some begged and pleaded not to go over to the afterlife because they had business to attend over amongst the living so I slapped them and told these people, "Get a grip you're dead deal with it fools!" So after doing my job I then went back to where my friend was. Just like that I asked him, "Ready to go elsewhere Jasay?"

A young child was juggling sharp knives with his hands.
As he begun to spin them faster and faster
his face had a bright smile on it.
He was amazed at his skill being realized.

Soon he began twisting around and adding extra
body motions while juggling the knives.
He began a sick laughter to go along
with what he was doing.
Just as he got over excited he tossed one of the
knives and a second one to go along with it.

Then while attempting to catch the two knives the first
one he missed and got impaled in the chest with it and
the second cut off his two hands as he began to die. Jasay
and I appeared before him as he came into his spirit form.
Jasay nodded at me and I said in our usual dark comedy
tone which we have throughout this tale, "So you had to
show off and looks like you killed yourself in the process
to be cool." I added, "Now you're really cool because
your dead and your body is cold cool shit eh kid?"

He began to cry at his own death by his
hand. I said to him, "Dammit kid, it's a
joke, don't be so overly sensitive shit!"
He sniffled and asked me, "Will I go to hell death?"
I answer him nicely and gently, "No son, it
was an accident so you will be forgiven."

"Let me take you to the afterlife, and guide you to heaven
where you will live out eternity peacefully." I added.

He stopped crying and gave his hand to me and we walked to heaven together while Jasay teleported out of the child's house and flew in the air and hovered over the people of this town where the child lived.

After I got back to Jasay, I told him, "Let's go send more people to the afterlife friend."

A man was preparing to leap off a
tall building to his death.
We stood on the ground at the bottom of the building
waiting for the fool to jump ending his life.
We overheard the idiot say because his life "was so
bad", "I'm ending my life because nobody cares about
me!" He gets ready to jump and Jasay and I shake our
heads at the foolish person's plight of killing himself.

He jumps and notices both me & Jasay looking
at him as he goes "splat" to the ground.
His head cracks open and his blood oozes onto the
sidewalk and the impact of hitting the ground at
that speed and pressure taken by his head connecting
with the hard ground killed him instantly.

We both see his spirit form, he then asks both
of us, "Am I dead death and little boy?"
Jasay laughs at him and I shake my head and
tell him, "Did you think jumping from a 6 story
building head first you would survive?" I added to
insult him, "You didn't make it pencil dick!"

He felt low and depressed from my comment and
asked, "Will I go to hell for killing myself?"
Jasay laughed even harder at the fool's stupid question. I
told him, "Are you of the Christian faith young man?"
He answered, "Yes death I am."
With that I answer sarcastically, "You will
meet your lord and your god!"
Due to his ignorance says, "That's great death!"

Horror Comedy Stories of John Omar Larnell Adams

I sigh and give him the truth, "You won't go to heaven foolish child, and you know who you will meet instead?" I added, "Lucifer and his demon minions to torture you severely in hell all for the reason of you killing yourself in a ridiculous manner isn't it great?"

The foolish man, who is saddened with his overall decision says, "I thought I would be let off the hook for this." He adds while crying, "I am doomed to be hurt for killing myself for eternity in hell am I not?"

Jasay and I laugh at his blubbering, I take him to hell with him kicking and begging not to go. Jasay falls over laughing at the fool's misery.

I come back an hour later and Jasay along with me go to another poor wretched soul's impending demise to witness and give the sad person's my decision to their soul's eternity.

A young teenage girl, spoiled rotten and an overall
good child, had stood in her bathroom with a bottle
of wine, a knife and three separate prescription
pill bottles. She was ready to commit suicide.

She drinks the wine first, and says to her self out
loud, "People hate me and treat me wrong so I want
to end my sad and awful life with these things!"
She begins to rapidly pop many of the pills
from the pill bottles and swallow them. She
takes the knife and slits one of her wrists.

Just as she goes about and does this Jasay and I appear
before her in the tub of the bathroom and she is sitting
on the bathroom's floor. She is scared because she sees
me, yells and asks, "What the fuck are death and a
midget doing with me?" She adds, "Am I already dead?"

I answer her, "You are close to death my dear, and if
my friend calls an ambulance you might be saved."
I then tell her, "It's not your time to die yet."

With this revelation she cheers up and
says to me, "Thank you death!"
I sigh and shake my head. Jasay says to her, "Instead
of popping pills like sweet tarts maybe you should
cherish life instead of B.S. it eh beautiful?"

She smiles and cries and says, "You are
very wise aren't you midget?"
Jasay looks at me and says, "Teenagers are brooding
and depressing individuals aren't they?" She

walks up to Jasay and kisses him on the lips and asks, "Want to have some sexy fun midget?"

I tell him, "Aren't you just the chick magnet Jasay?" He answers, "Shut up good friend!" He adds, "Every teenage girl and woman and elderly woman think I am a midget man."

She while high off the pills and drunk off the wine tends to her cut on the left wrist she cut earlier. As it stops bleeding she removes her clothes and gets bare ass naked in front of us. She then says, "It's time for sexy time midget!" I leave Jasay to his sex with the teenage girl. After all the moaning and bumping in the bathroom is over, Jasay appears wide eyed and reeking of vagina. He says, "Let's call an ambulance for that vixen good buddy now!" He adds, "Then let's get the hell out of here!" We call the ambulance. The girl waves at us and blows a kiss at Jasay. He blushes and both of us teleports out of her home and we go to our next sad soul.

I stumbled across a conflict in a war torn country.
I decided to watch it play it's self out.
As the bullets flew by, I saw rebels getting hit with
the bullets or getting blown up by rockets or grenades
or even missiles. There were bodies dropping and
Jasay was a bit appalled at the carnage these humans
were doing to each other. He flew over them in the
air watching as I was still on the ground surveying
all this horrendous happenings going down.

As this battle ended and both sides were killed off, I
saw them in spirit forms all next to their bodies. Jasay
flew down after the spirited battle ended and saw the
dead bodies scattered around. Blood pouring out of
them and pieces of limbs placed everywhere. They
had bullet holes all over them, some blown to nothing
but bits of skin and bones from the explosions.

I told Jasay, "War brings out the savage beast in
mortals and these beasts ripped each other to
shreds over their territory and couldn't agree."
Jasay added, "The beasts had to be put down as if
they were diseased and their owners (their weapons)
had more control over them until their light was put
out." "To bad they went off their leashes and "got
into the trash can" so to speak eh good buddy?"

I told him, "Well put and eloquently said good
friend, you're getting better at dark humor."
As he said this and I answered him, the rebels all looked at
us in disbelief and were saddened to be dead. They asked
me, "Why did this happen to us?" We both looked at each

other and laughed at them, just then I asked a question
to the "tools", "Using guns, grenades, missiles and rockets
to settle a dispute would really end greatly right?"

They were ashamed in the violent deaths and still in
disbelief and had started weeping uncontrollably in
a funny and sad way, Jasay spit on the ground and
shook his head. I began to explain their futures to all
these insane idiots, "Since you all killed one another in
hatred and didn't repent for your past sins and did this
with malice, guess where you fuckers will be going?"
They stopped crying and asked, "Where to death?"

I answered them with a sly and devious smile, "To
hell of course you wretched and poor souls!"
They screamed loudly in protest, "Please no death!"
They added, "We don't want eternal damnation please
reconsider?" I waved my hand opened the portal to hell
and took them all with my power and with music to force
them to go into hell unwillingly. They screamed and
couldn't fight the music to drive them into their eternity.
The portal closed and I took them all to hell to face their
torture and misery for eternity with demons and Lucifer.

Jasay waited patiently and I returned and
we went elsewhere to find other disturbing
people who were destined to die or let off
because it wasn't time for them to die yet.

We stumbled across a bunker, which in
turn became a tomb for the soldiers because
of nerve gas being let inside of it.

I went in first to see if it was safe for Jasay to see the
horrible tragedy and death of these dumb soldiers
who walked into their own deaths by nerve gas.
After opening the door the leftover gas came filtering
out, Jasay stepped out of the way and flew into the air.
While he avoided the nerve gas remnants, I came out of
the bunker. I started laughing eerily at Jasay's plight of
using a near mortal body which can't take nerve gas.

I asked him, "Why don't you let the gas disperse
and I will wait for you to join me in looking at
the dead dumbass soldiers alright friend?"

He answered very loudly, "Alright I will
wait for it to disperse good buddy!"
Once the gas completely dissipated Jasay flew down
and came into the bunker with me. He said, "Well it
smells of mortal death right?" He adds, "A great smell
and sight "for everyone" right?" I laughed at his sarcasm.
Then I said, "Only humans and other mortal beings try
to ignore the dead, only a select few can stomach it."

The look of terror on the dead bodies' faces
would turn the bravest human's stomach.
They looked completely frightened and we saw
their spirits in the bunker crying like babies. I told
them, "Since you all didn't repent and only thought
of yourselves instead of trying to get out together

and all the killing you soldiers have done gets you
all a one way ticket to… I added, "Who wants to
guess where you lowly bastards are going to?"

One of the blubbering ghosts of the soldiers asked
while the others were in sheer fright and the sight
of me, "Are we going to hell Death?" I answer
the brains of their war mongering set with, "Yes
smart guy that's where you lowlifes are going."

Jasay laughs at their pleas and cries to not be led into hell.
He tells them, "Maybe fighting and killing each
other to the death for your "so called" country isn't
really worth the trip to hell huh numb nuts?"

They shake their sad and shameful heads no
at Jasay. I open the portal and play the music
to move them forcefully into hell. The song
is the classical piece Danse Macabre.

It forces the dead and spirits to forcefully dance as
we go to Heaven, Hell, Limbo or Purgatory.

As the portal closes, Jasay awaits my return. When I
return, then tell him let's go. I then ask him, "Since
you're in that body Jasay, do you want something
to eat?" I tell him let's fly to a fast food restaurant
for him which we do he gets a kids meal and I
watch him eat it, once he finished we go fly off to
the shock of the patrons who see us both fly off.

While Jasay flew in the air, I flew next to him as we joked about the events we had seen up to now. We got to a nation of starving people because of a corrupt government. While we were in this African nation, some of the starving people including children, adults, the elderly; teenagers and babies begin to fall over and slowly die.

Jasay sees them come near him because they smell food on him. Once they came over to grab at him to see if he would give them food. Jasay pushed them down and from the shock of the physical attack by him begin to die in front of him and me. Some of the soldiers from the corrupt government within this country begin to take whatever is left from the villagers.

They spot Jasay and they also see me, they get scared and raise their guns at us. I say to Jasay, "Looks like we might have to make death for these mortals." He nods and as he does, the soldiers try to open fire on us. Jasay mini teleports with ultra fast movement he learned from living in Asia and training with some of them there. He then appears behind the soldiers and begins to turn the soldiers head around completely killing him and hitting the other soldiers in the chest hard enough to burst their hearts.

I just touch them and they die.
After we dispatched the soldiers, their spirits show up without the guns they all had. Scared they speak African which Jasay and I understand. We tell them in their language they are dead. I explain to them for their dastardly deeds they are on a one

way trip to hell. I quickly open the portal to hell
and play Danse Macabre for them to uncontrollably
dance to the afterlife they will be going to.

I tell the spirits of the former starving people,
"I will be back to take them into heaven."
They nod and I nod at Jasay who nods back at me.
I take the soldiers to hell. Then come back and lead
the ghosts of the starving villagers to heaven. After
finishing Jasay and I leave and go elsewhere.

There was a dictator in a South American country, was being raided by a militant group within the nation. As his men were being slaughtered, he began the grave task of setting up retaliation for his soldiers deaths by what was left of them to pick off the militant group.

Jasay and I watched from a distance as this vile murder and bloodshed went on. Jasay said to me as we floated above this set of killings going on, "These dictators get their power to set all of their people free and let them live accordingly yet they give all of the people a reign of tyranny." He added, "Ironic they get the fate of death for trying to give freedom and instead die a violent death and go to hell right good friend?"

I just nodded as we watched more of this carnage unfold. As his leftover soldiers killed some of the rebel faction which had wanted to go and overthrow this tyrant. The dictator ran off to hide in his "special room" while his so called cronies were working to dispatch the rebel army.

In Spanish the fool began to lament what was happening asking to himself, "Why me?" Jasay and I laughed at him. He thought there would be no repercussions to his evil deeds to the people he made downtrodden and suffer because of his excess and tastes. After all the killing stopped once all the soldiers in his employ were dead.

They stormed his room and shot him from the beginning of the door in the head. He fell dead as blood trickled from the head shot onto the ground.

The rebel army cheered in victory of killing the tyrant and his army of cronies. They exited the estate of the dictator. Jasay shook his head and stated, "This foolishness keeps repeating itself in all forms on this worthless planet!"

I told him, "Yeah it is just my job gets it's quota from these fools dieing or getting killed some sort of way though Jasay." We laughed at my statement. The spirits of the dictator and his army came near us. I spoke to them in Spanish and asked them, "Guess where you shitheads are going?" In English they all stated, "No please!" The Danse Macabre music played and they forcefully danced as I took them to hell. Jasay waited for me yet again.

Once I returned we flew to the next place of death to these poor wretched souls of earthlings.

A man speeding down a residential street, and sees a
cat walking across the street and swerves out of the
way of the feline and hits a fire hydrant. Flies through
his windshield from the impact and goes head first
into the ground breaking his neck and dieing because
of the action. Jasay says to me, "Well good friend it
looks like speed does kill." I laugh at his dark humor.

We both see the man as a spirit and he pops his neck
back into place. He asks us, "Am I really dead?"
I answer him sarcastically, "No dumbass you're
alive." He then comes to the latter realization he
stated earlier. He begins to cry like a crybaby. Jasay
looks at him dumbfounded because of the guy
getting so emotional like a guy or girl who had
their lover break up with them for no reason.

I sigh and tell the sap, "Look so you are dead buddy." I
added, "Stop crying would you please?" He slowly starts
to stop and says, "I am sorry Death it just happened so
suddenly you know and it is hard to process because one
minute I am alive the next second there it is I'm dead."

My scythe begins to glow, and I begin to tell this
sad person what he really doesn't want to hear,
"Looks like you go to heaven for a while and
they will decide what happens to your sad and
terrible soul you depressing piece of shit!"

The guy begins to cry again and Jasay says, "This is really
sad good buddy, take him away he is starting to make
me feel sorry for being a stupid head in the first place."

I tell my friend, "Yeah, he makes me feel bad for him being so ignorant and I will take him now!" The Danse Macabre classical piece plays again and he forcefully dances while I take him to where they will decide his fate.

Jasay waits up for me then afterwards both of us fly away and we both leave again.

An old couple was having sex and is going at it hard and
fast, which is unbelievable considering their advanced age.
Jasay and I stood in their bedroom watching not
quite appalled or excited. Both were saying, "It's
good to me baby!" Just then it was because their
heart rates were going at the maximum beats. The
two of them died on the spot after climaxing.

The two elderly peoples' spirits appeared before us stark
naked, wrinkly, and lastly liver spotted with sagging skin.

I said, "Oh that's some nasty shit!" Jasay said, "I might be
blind for life at this horrible and nasty site before my eyes!"
Then the two old people glance over and see
their dead, naked bodies with their eyes wide
open and say, "Holy hell we're dead!"
I tell them, "No shit you naked,
wrinkly and sagging geniuses!"
Jasay added, "You died doing something you loved
which killed you." He adds, "How do you oldies feel?"

They turn in front and seeing their wrinkly genitals in
our faces, we go, "Please hug each other or something
please now!" Still disgusted at this horrid sight of
old naked wrinkly bodies, the two hug each other to
appease us. Knowing they have both of us more than
horrified turn in front exposing their genitalia again
and ask, "Do our naked bodies scare you that much?"
They flash sly devilish smiles at our discomfort.

I try to cover my eye sockets by holding my hand
over it. To my chagrin I see through my bones their

naked and twisted bodies. I say, "Shit man this is disgusting!" I tell Jasay, "This sickens me." I add, "How about you my pal?" He tells me, "Most definitely!"

I then turn to the sexual pre-deviants and tell them to my delight, "Since you're dead, I will take you heaven and your fates will be decided from there because I don't want to deal with your nasty old asses anymore!"

The Danse Macabre starts and the old people unwillingly dance and are moving themselves into the portal so I can be rid of them finally. Jasay claps as I lead them into the portal with the music. The portal disappears as Jasay waits for me again. After getting back, I ask him, "That was a bit much wasn't it?" He nods and we disappear again.

A man who had too many drinks at a bar
stumbles onto the sidewalk and walks up it.
The intoxication is a bit much for him, and he
throws up on the sidewalk ahead of him. He begins
to move forward a bit still completely drunk.

He falls forward and hits the concrete very hard.
Knocking himself out and cracking his head open.
Blood begins to ooze from his head, he then lets
out a guttural moan and dies on the spot.

He stands over his body and begins to ponder
where he went wrong and became an alcoholic
asking himself, "Why did I ever start drinking?" He
shakes his head and gets ready to start crying now.
Jasay and I appear before the dead guy's spirit.

I begin to imitate him drinking at the bar and coming
outside and falling to the ground and dieing. He was
not amused and starts to cry. Jasay tells him, "Looks
like hitting the bottle paid off didn't it buddy?"

Hurt by my dark humor and Jasay's sarcasm, he begins
to whine saying, "Why do you all have to make light
of my death?" I ask him, "You can't see the humor in
all this silly shit you had done to end up dead being a
glutton for the liquor and beer and dumbly falling on
your face and head dieing as a result huh stupid ass?"

Him still crying says loudly while still blubbering,
"It's not funny you two I am dead damn it!"

I tell and ask Jasay, "He's a sad person who really
can't take humor or a joke can't he Jasay?"
He tells me, "Obviously not good friend."
He adds, "He has no humor for the macabre
or morbid despite his situation now."

I tell the sad and crying fool, "Guess where
you're going since you didn't repent and was
a glutton and basically killed yourself?"
The foolish man answers by asking,
"Where am I going Death?"
I answer him with a laugh, "To Hell
of course foolish mortal!"

He cries even harder saying, "No please
Death!" He adds, "Not there please!"
The portal opens and the Danse Macabre classical piece
plays again and he unwillingly dances like the others
as I lead him to hell, Jasay looks at the guy and laughs
at him as he is lead into hell. He waits for my return
and once I got back to where Jasay was we left again.

A newscaster on that said local news show, and she berates everyone on the set of this show before going back on air. While most think of her as a deranged cunt, they hope good things happen for her such as she gets sent to another news station way out of the area where their lovely newscast was filmed. She gets angrier and madder. As she does her heart begins tightening from the stress of being overworked. She feels chest pains and asks for water. The pain persists. As the news goes back on air, she tries to fake niceness and joy as her segment goes on she feels the pain in her chest go unabated. After this happens she grabs her chest as the pain gets harder and more painful for her.

Finally the pain hits a fever pitch and becomes so unbearable she feels her life begin to fade. After the pain goes into overdrive and can't take it anymore, she says to everyone in the area through the television, "Shit I am dying!" After saying this she dies and collapses on the news table. The camera crew and producer of the show go over to check the body. They put a technical difficulties screen on to shield young viewers from her dead body on the air. The damage had been done.

Calls went into the news station. People were very upset at her language and the fact she died on air seen by young children and everyone else. Jasay and I were in the newscast room. The female newscaster's spirit appeared before us. Jasay waved at her. I told my buddy, "Don't be friendly with this silly and mean bitch Jasay."

He said, "Right good buddy." To the wonder bitch
realizing she was in spirit form after seeing her body
looked over by her co workers says, "I can't believe
I am ghost and see Death and a pretty midget."
Jasay tells her, "Actually angry lady I am a boy."
She says, "Sure you're a boy you pretty midget." He
shakes his head and says to me in a mock game show
host voice, "Tell her what she's won good sir!"

With a look of shock on her face asks me, "What's the
midget mean by that?" I laugh and tell her, "What he
means is you're going to hell missy!" I add, "That's what
you have won on the game show of "your death!"

The portal opens and the Danse Macabre music plays
and she uncommonly dances where she is forced to and
dances into the portal to be sent to hell for anger and pure
disdain for humanity on a daily basis and her vanity as
top billing on the news show and being full of herself.

Jasay laughed at her dancing and the portal closed. The
coworkers wondered why he was laughing and the portal
reopened and I appear the crew and everyone working
there were very frightened. Jasay tried to reassure them.
Some of them fainted. We both left after all this mayhem.

A local high school athlete, who was practicing
has the most horrible misfortune when
Something terrible happened to him.
While doing practice drills with his team after the
coach had asked him to do extra drills since he
needed to step his game up to the champion level to
have the team take the state championship and so
the athlete could make the All American Team.

As the teenager was getting ready to finish out his senior
year at the high school, some trouble began to have a
terrible effect on his body in the most serious way.
He had begun to shake violently and
began throwing up repeatedly.
He began to have strong convulsions. He stopped
for a second and his coach, and then all of the
team showed concern for him. He came to and
become his usual fit self. As he reassured those
around him he was fine something else started.

He began to feel hot and began to sweat profusely,
the nausea came back and he felt a migraine come on
and his heart sped up, lastly feeling chest pains.
He fell to the ground, grabbed his chest and said to his
teammates and coach, "Call an ambulance now!"
After saying this, he died quickly and in
a fit of pain and painless things.

Jasay and I appeared before his spirit, he saw
the two of us and felt frightened because
of the realization he was now dead.

Just then, Jasay and I to break the ice said to him
in a joking manner with dark comedy overtones
state, "Trying to be the best in every way and look
what happened because of your hard work and
pushing your body to its full limit, you died!"

He looked appalled at our humor and gulped
suddenly. He asked me, "Death where am I headed
to now that me dying has sent me where?"
I looked at him and said boldly, "Since you basically
overworked yourself maybe for all your work that
the place where your soul ends up is heaven." I
added, "You did something foolish looks like you
have people looking out for you in the afterlife."

He looked happier than before and said to me, "Thank
you Death!" Adding in saying while shaking my hand,
"You have no idea how much this means to me."
With that I opened the portal and the Danse Macabre
music played again, he had forcefully danced to
the music and was led by me to his destination
of where his soul would find eternal peace. The
portal closes and Jasay waits for me to come back
and go to the next poor soul who has died.
As I come back Jasay is awaiting me, the coach and
teammates of the soul I took away notice him and as soon
of the fact I appeared the group fainted thinking they
were next to go over into the afterlife. Jasay and I laugh
at the fools and disappear elsewhere to the next place.

A gymnast at a gymnastics competition, the female
gymnast begins a floor routine. She begins her run
and does a forward flip, not judging her trajectory
she noticed her head going into the ground as she
lands headfirst. The impact breaks her neck and
her spine pops through the skin where her back was
in place. Some blood from the spine going through
the skin leaks onto the competition floor.

The audience, her coaches, teammates and
judges are appalled, shocked and horrified
at the gruesome sight of this tragedy.
The teenage gymnast's spirit stands dumbfounded
at what happened to her self in this terrible
moment. She sees me and Jasay before her.

Crying hysterically, she asks me,
"Death am I really dead now?!"
To make her feel at ease, I then tell her, "Yes you did
die from underestimating yourself." I add, "Sorry
my dear." Jasay tells her to make her laugh, "All
that practice tumbling and flipping, lastly landing
and you end up killing yourself, tragic huh?"

The young teenage girl looks in shock at what Jasay said to
her in disbelief of a boy making light of her tragic demise.
Angry a bit, she asks of him, "How could you make such
a macabre joke about this horrible travesty you midget?!"
He tells her, "Cheer up angry girl!" He adds to
make her feel better, "At least you won't suffer
anymore by people making you over exert yourself
practicing and not eating basically killing yourself

to be a gymnast anymore, you will be in eternal
peace away from suffering what you felt in life."

She stops crying and walks over and kisses
Jasay on the lips at his revelation to her.
After doing this she says to him, "For a midget who tells
macabre jokes you are pretty wise and quite cute!"
Jasay, sort of embarrassed by her comment
says, "Thank you pretty girl!"

She smiles at him. I clear my throat and tell her, "Now
that you got a boy crush on him, it is time for you to go
over into the afterlife my dear." The portal opens and
the Danse Macabre music plays and the young teenage
girl dances forcefully while this is going on people
come to clear her body away and her family distraught
cry and moan at the sight of their loved one dead by
accident. Once she entered the portal I followed behind
her and Jasay waits for me. He is seen by everyone at the
competition. After a few moments I return scaring the
daylights out of the people at this gymnastics event. Most
faint, while others are horrified that their death is next.

I nod to Jasay and he nods back at me. We then
disappear to the next place where someone dies.

A group of young adults on a drug bender, who are all feeling very high and calm find later on that they should have never done this many drugs in the first place.

While some were snorting cocaine, others were smoking Marijuana, some were smoking PCP, the others in this drug fueled bender smoked methamphetamine; some were smoking hashish, others were popping pills and opiates, others were shooting up heroin, some took ecstasy, others took hallucinogenic mushrooms; some took Quaaludes, some smoked opium; others took peyote, others did mescaline, others were dropping LSD, some were huffing ether, gasoline, aerosol cans and Freon, smoking salvia, popping caffeine tablets, drinking codeine, sipping cough syrup, using asthma inhalers; eye drops, etc.

Once they all were beginning to overdose or having drug induced heart attacks, they began dropping like flies. Men, women, teenagers; the middle aged, young adults; the elderly and children all dying suddenly from their trying to get the highest they could all get in an exploration of excess.

Once all these stupid and poor souls were finally dead and shit on themselves or threw up or even both, their spirits came out of their husks which were alive a while ago.

Jasay and I appear before their sad and shocked spirits, I open a window to keep Jasay's lungs from being infected by these idiots so called "fun". They ask me in unison, "So Death is it true that we are all really dead from all this partying?"

Shaking my head, I answer the fools by saying,
"Yes you ignorant and stupid pieces of shit all of
you are now dead from your apparent excess."

Crying from all of them ensues, Jasay to lighten
the mood tells them in a joke, "Guess there
really aren't enough drugs to kill yourself with
fast enough to use huh good people?"

They call my friend an asshole and for that discrepancy,
I open the portal immediately and the Danse Macabre
music plays and all the fools dance forcefully. I tell
them, "For insulting my best friend here you get to be
judged now!" I add, "Onto the afterlife for you dumb
pieces of shit!" They holler loudly, "No please not this
Death!" As they all dance in unison to the classical
piece and go into the portal Jasay laughs at them as
they cry hysterically for being led to be judged for their
ending of their lives without warning by drug usage.

After the portal closes, a few moments go by I
appear and Jasay and I go onto our next place
for a poor soul dying or about to die.

A comedian who is snorting a lot of cocaine before doing his comedy set, stops after his last bump of cocaine gets up his nose and gets ready to near the stage to deliver jokes. He gets introduced and begins his comedy set, he says to the crowd, "You know I haven't died on stage in a long time, let's hope there is no premature death this time." With that he feels his heart beating at an even faster rate than usual, he grabs his chest and says, "Oh shit I am really dying here!" The audience begins to laugh at him thinking he is doing physical comedy with his joke to simulate death. Unbeknownst to them this is no joke or physical comedy. He is really dying this time in reality and not from getting any laughs at his jokes during a standup comedy set.

He keels over on his back and lets out a grumble and dies instantly. The MC goes over and tells him, "Stop playing around man and get up." He adds to the seemingly dead comedian, "I am serious man get up!" He sort of kicks him in the side. He doesn't move and says, "Call an ambulance he might really be dead here!" The audience shocked and horrified by this turn of events gasps or screams at the morbid scene.

Jasay and I appear before the comedian's spirit, he looks surprised to see me and Jasay in front of him. He states to me, "Did I really die this time death?" I look at Jasay who looks at me and Jasay says, "You tell the joke this time good buddy!" So I smile before the dead comedian and tell him, "You had a big fear of dying again on stage from bad jokes told and you told a good morbid joke and sure enough you have "bit the big one" and died for real this time literally!"

Hurt and depressed, the comedian stumbles back from my mentioning of his death says, "Will I be going to heaven or hell Death?" Jasay and I giggle at the fool giving himself a drug induced heart attack from getting rid of "stage jitters". So I ask him, "Guess what is going to happen now?" He asks, "Now what?" He adds, "You two were laughing at me a second ago."

The portal opens and the Danse Macabre plays again, I tell him, "Now you idiot who thinks he is funny you will be judged where you go in the afterlife." The comedian dances uncontrollably and forcefully. He enters the portal and I follow as it closes Jasay waits for me still.

Jasay stands there and the audience wonders what a midget is doing in the comedy club. I appear again and scare all of the people in the comedy club and the ambulance even the policemen and women. Jasay and I laugh at the people as they faint. We disappear to go over to the next poor dead soul.

A musician who casually practices his instrument,
which is a saxophone on a daily basis, begins
to feel really numb all of a sudden.
He looks around breathing very hard and begins to see
the world tilt in his vision. He gets light headed and
slowly just surely he feels the life in his body leaving him.

So just like that he dies of over exertion and
fatigue in the most extreme of ways.
His body slumps over and falls to the ground
of his practice space in his house.
After he realizes that his soul just left his
body, himself in spirit form stares at his body
in amazement that died so suddenly.

Jasay and I appear before his living soul. He
asks me, "So after all of the life that I have
lived now I am dead right Death?"
I answer him with a calm manner of voice,
"Yes Mr. Musician, you are very dead."
Jasay to lighten the mood says to the newly deceased
man, "You knew music soothed the most savage beast,
only to realize your music could not soothe the beast that
is before you." He adds, "He's here and he is Death!"

The musician was not amused by Jasay's joke asks of
him, "You like the morbid jokes don't you midget?"
Jasay unbiased says to him, "Yes I like them and maybe
you should have taken longer rests from blowing into
your saxophone and also you would be alive now."

The musician now angry begins to charge at Jasay, I open the portal in a quick fashion. The music of Danse Macabre starts, the musician starts dancing forcefully.

I waved my finger and begin a tissing session with the musician then tell him, "No hitting him mortal, you will be taken to the other side so that you can be judged."
With that the musician now scared because
of his involuntary dancing is lead through
the portal to where he will be judged.
Jasay waits for me to return so we
can mock another dead soul.

I return, and then we go onto the next soul
which I will lead into the afterlife.

A highly stressed out stock broker on Wall
Street begins to feel a sharp and strong pain in
his chest as he trades stocks for NASDAQ.
After a long night of drinking and sex with
hookers and strippers at the strip club he feels
the effects of his hedonism and gluttony so he
could have fun before work starts again.
The pain in his chest grows as he still
feels the alcohol in his system.

Some of his coworkers show no concern for him
as they continue trading themselves. As the pain
becomes more intense, he grabs at his chest. Some of
the people trading ask him if he is alright and he says
to them, "Only slight chest pains, I will be fine."

Just then the final push of chest pains hits harder
than all the other pain he has felt all morning
long. His vision gets blurry, he has a head spin,
after that he gets nauseous not enough to throw
up just an ever going sickness in his stomach.
He says as the pain starts killing him, "Oh Shit!"

Just then he falls backward dead on the floor.
Jasay and I stand and look at this hapless fool.
His spirit looks at the two of us and we tell him
in unison as a joke to lighten up the mood and
this dead idiot, "Looks like this stressful work,
partying and screwing random pays off until you
die from the strain and excess right buddy?"

He was not amused at this and seemed to be more worried as more people began to scramble as to what they could do with this dumbasses body now that he is dead.

He asks me, "Why did I have to die now Death?" I answer him, "You didn't treasure life or see it was precious in each moment." I added, "So it was your time to "bite the big one" so to speak." Still in disbelief, he looks very sad now. Jasay nods at me and I decide to tell the poor sap one more thing, "Well sir it looks like you are going to be lead into the afterlife now." Opening the portal, the music of Danse Macabre plays and the former stock broker starts dancing forcefully and as he does I lead him to where he will now spend eternity.

Jasay laughs very hard at the stock broker dancing forcefully, I laugh at the stock broker's bad dancing as well. He looks scared as he is forced to dance from the music. He goes into the portal and I follow him and finally get him to his destination to be judged.

After getting back to Jasay we go onto the next poor soul who is dead or about to die.

We go to a cabbie in New York City, who won't let
minorities in his cab, begins to stop for someone and
doesn't know that he is picking up a black man in makeup
disguised as a Caucasian male businessman. He doesn't
notice the sound of a pistol in the briefcase he is carrying
to get revenge on the cabbie for not picking him up before.

The cabbie slumps over and his blood trickles down
onto the floor of the cab and he falls forward on
the steering wheel and then blares the horn.
He gets away from his body, the assailant or
murderer whichever you want to call this person
who did a dastardly version of "revenge served
cold" gets out of the cab and runs off.
So his spirit gets in the passenger seat, and
we both see him and his dead body.

The spirit moves through the door and
stands before Jasay and me.
He asks, "Are you Death?" I answer him,
"Yes and you are dead, killed by a disgruntled
customer who was not picked up you cabbie."

He then asks, "Where am I going to Death?" The answer
he got from me was, "It solely depends on those who will
judge you and where you yourself will be going." I added,
"They told me I was too judgmental, so I have to let the
others judge where your soul will go for now and forever."

Jasay says to him, "Looks like letting people stand the
elements or not getting where they need to go cost you
your life for you negligence and mean intentions eh?"

The cabbie says to me, "Your little friend has a serious and macabre way to look at things even though he makes serious and macabre jokes."

I tell the cabbie, "No need to worry about my best friend here he is an observer and a keen one on human beings." Then I added to ease the thoughts of the cabbie, "Now that all the formalities are done, let's get you to wherever place in the afterlife that you will reside in." The portal opens and the Danse Macabre music plays and the cabbie had forcefully begun dancing to the classical piece.

After he went through the portal, I followed him and took him to his final destination where he would spend his eternity at.

Jasay waited patiently for my return and when I did he laughed and asked, "Are we going to another hapless idiot or fool where you send them to their fate for eternity good buddy?" I told him, "You know it great friend of mine."

In Chicago, during a street gang fight, two rival
gang factions fight each other, some are stabbing one
another, the others beating on and stomping each other.
While lastly some of these rival gangs pull out guns.
As a treat for their rivals some of the smart ones put
silencers on the handguns. As the shots ring out people
fall down dead and the rival gang factions scatter.

While both sides now have 10 each lying dead and
lifeless, their spirits arise from their bodies.
Jasay and I are waiting for these dead gang
members so I can lead them to where they can
spend eternity either happy or in misery.
Some of them recognize Jasay and asks him, "So
John-John what are you doing with Death?" He
answers them, "I am just hanging out with him, he's
my best friend and we have known each other way
before humans or this solar system or this universe
or any universe for that matter was created."

Shocked by my friends revelation they look dumbfounded
and scared then ask me, "Death is John-John really
some kind of god or something because he looks like
a little kid or boy and that's what we know him as."
I laugh and answer the deceased mortal by saying, "It
is true and maybe you should have known about him
before befriending him or initiating him into one of
your street gangs and putting him into the kind of
danger you put yourselves into and ended up dead."

I added, "Now that you all are dead, I will lead your
poor souls into the afterlife, you might all end up in

hell just for killing each other and other people just
because they are in different gangs then yourselves."
Now that these young men realized they had died
for nothing begin to think maybe all of them
could have chosen a different path in life.

I open the portal and the Danse Macabre music starts
and the hapless gang members start to dance forcefully
and uncontrollably. Some holler at Jasay and ask him,
"John-John please help us!" They add while whining so
sadly, "We don't want to go into hell convince Death
that we shouldn't go there come on John-John!"
Jasay explains to them, "I can't convince him not
to take you there, you are dead now and his job is
to lead dead souls over to the afterlife where they
spend eternity in damnation or in peace."

With that the gang members dance still as the music
forces them to dance into the portal as I lead them to
their destination the portal closes. Jasay shaking his
head, he then awaits for me to return. When I did get
back to my best friend he smiles and we get ready for
our next unfortunate soul going to the afterlife.

John Omar Larnell Adams

In a federal prison, there is an intense prison riot going on. Some of the prisoners have taken the prison guards hostage, some are burning mattresses and others are trying to tear the bars off the windows of their prison cell. There are big group fights where the prisoners who are gay or straight or even bisexual or lastly transgender are either getting beaten to death or stabbed with shanks or their throats slit by opposite members of each group mentioned within the prison population.

Now that all this going on, also prison
guards are being killed.

Soon the national guard was called in, they took aim at the prisoners rioting and other surviving prisoners in this riot and shot them all to death after the governor called them in to contain or even kill the prisoners if need be.

The army's men finish off the remaining
prisoners, afterwards take their weapons and
fall out in synchronization marching as if they
were angels of death had been casting "the
end" for these troubled and evil prisoners.
With that the prisoners bodies quickly died and their
spirits were now in full sight of Jasay and me.

As we saw these horrible degenerates of human existence dead and their lifeless bodies with the look of shock that they were killed so suddenly, swiftly and with no mercy. They ask, "Why did we have to die now Death?" I answer these pieces of shit saying, "For all the anal rape in here, the bad behavior and your actions in

136

society which got you all here why does it surprise
you all that for every little action you did there
would be a reaction to it huh dumb shits?"

Whining now and moaning, Jasay laughs at them all. I
couldn't stand the sight of these fuckheads any longer.
So I opened the portal in haste to get rid of these sad
mortals whose deeds render them only to go into hell for
eternity and face misery, dread and torture for eternity.

The portal opens and the Danse Macabre plays and
the former alive prisoners started forcefully dancing.
As they danced Jasay and I laughed at their horrid
looks on their faces as they being led into the portal
dancing uncontrollably. I followed after them. The
portal closed and Jasay waited for me as usual.

When I returned we disappeared and went elsewhere
to the next tragic incident causing people to die.

Two people are bungee jumping off a bridge.
As they get rid of the fear of jumping from a high
place to a lower place for thrills, they smile at each
other the husband and wife do to each other.
While the instructor gives them "the
nod" everything was ready to go.
The couple wanted to bungee jump for their
first year anniversary bucket list.

As they get into position to jump, the
instructor gives them all a 1,2,3,4 count.
They then jump off the platform to bungee
jump. As they descend the couple didn't realize
this would be their last moments together.

The mechanism holding them from completely
free falling would stick and as they continued
falling more tension hit the mechanism.
Way before hitting the ground the couple got
an intense adrenaline rush from the jump.
They hit that ground very hard head first. The instructor
and other people waiting to jump were shocked,
disturbed and appalled at the tragedy they all just seen.

As their bodies dangle and blood leaks from their eyes,
ears, mouths and noses. Also their necks were broken and
their hips protruding through the skin of these sad people.
Jasay and I saw their spirits staring at us. We waved
at the two of them which made them uneasy and
unwilling to accept their deaths from misadventure.

Jasay tells them jokingly, "Looks like thrills take
you out whether you speed in a car or jump from a
plane or off a bridge with bungee cord." He adds,
"Was it enough to die from your fun people?"

They are both appalled that a little boy's sense of humor
is so sarcastic, and macabre or really morbid. I begin to
talk it over with the two of them, "Well happy or dead
couple, you two died and it looks like its time for you
both to be judged where you will spend eternity."

I laugh and tell them, "Here we go now dead people
who love thrills!" The portal opens and the Danse
Macabre plays and the former living couple dance to
the classical piece forcefully and uncontrollably then
go into the portal. I go after the dancing fools. The
portal closes and Jasay still waits for my return.

I get back and we go to our next dead soul
to be lead into the afterlife by me.

A bubbly man working with a mobile buzz saw in his
garage cutting wood for a project has this happen.
As he pushes the wood through the rotating saw
he thought that he was paying close attention
to safety. It is just more sawdust and wood
came up even more than usual this time.

While his vision was obstructed, he didn't notice he
cut off both his forearms with both hands as well.
He let out a loud yell, "AHHHHHHH!"
He was bleeding very profusely and quickly, the
blood kept flowing and flowing in a rush.

He began to feel lightheaded and felt cold.
Just then his life flashes before his eyes and he
says, "I didn't live a bad life at all." With that he
dies and his spirit comes out of his body.

He sees the two of us shaking our head at this fool who
put his project ahead of his own safety who killed himself
by accident like the stupid couple who liked thrills.
He asks, "So I am dead huh Death?"
I answer him, "Yes you idiot the fact is your
dumbass didn't look at what you were doing cut off
your forearms and hands with them bled to death
and now you are before me aren't you lucky?"

Jasay says to him, "Looks the wood got you cut for trying
to reform into some sort of silly project you wanted to do
instead of doing something that would benefit humanity."
The dead fool's spirit seemed distraught we laid into him
like this. Just to make him feel worse I opened the portal

on purpose this time and the Danse Macabre plays and
he danced forcefully and uncontrollably like the others.

After I followed after him to take him to his
destination for eternity Jasay laughed at the sheer
terror on this fools face dancing without himself
really trying to dance. I laughed at him too. The
portal closed and my friend waited for me as usual.
After returning to where Jasay stood I nodded at him
and we went then disappeared to another sad soul to
take over into their final destination for eternity.

A ballerina performing during a ballet concert was doing her pirouettes and leaps while performing. She was graceful, clever and cunning in all sense of the word. Turning and having a complete rhythm while interpreting this music in the background giving theme and majesty to this high visual and audio art.

While at the height of this ballet, she does a kick out and scale then goes for a leap. Unbeknownst to her this would be her final curtain call. As she leapt the lady didn't count on landing awkwardly and downright wrong. After trying to land she hit the ground making her brain smash up inside of her skull squishing her brain and killing her instantly.

The audience sick to this terror and terrible sight of her demise caused many of the female patrons of this ballet to faint. Blood trickled down the ballerina's nose onto the floor as her body had lain there dead.

The sight was something to see if you loved ballet that is. It is almost tragic she died, almost. We stood there and saw her spirit, she gasped at the sight of me. She smiled at Jasay though. It seems women and girls have a soft spot for him.

She asked, "So now that I am dead, you take me somewhere right Death?" I nod at her question. The dead woman then asks, "Do I get to fool around with this midget here with the pretty long hair?"

Annoyed, I say to her, "You're being led into your
destination for eternity, no you are not getting
in the pants of my best friend here girlie!"
She then groans a bit and tells me, "You're absolutely
no fun Death and I just wanted to get a little
before spending eternity without getting laid."

I answer her, "You mortals have too many
off putting needs for carnal desire not
intended for mating and procreation!"

Pissed off at her request still I open the portal, and
say to her, "Now you will dance without smashing
your stupid brain to mush you stupid ass mortal!"

The music of Danse Macabre plays and she unwillingly
dances and goes into the portal and Jasay looks a
little sad to see her go away. I follow after her and
lead the horny chick into her eternal destination.
The portal closes and Jasay waits again.

I return and tell him, "We have only a few more
errands of dead people to for me to lead them into
the afterlife for your day spent with me at my job
here." He goes, "Fine with me good buddy!" We
then go after my next dead target or targets.

During a play at a theatre, all the actors are
handling themselves performing a 20th Century
play and something goes amiss….
The cast was on fire, the lines were delivered at a
professional and top notch rate. The acting was
believable and great. Everyone was giving it their all.

Then it all went to "hell in a hand basket."
Suddenly during a scene showing a change in the
direction of the play a terrible thing happened as a big
time stage actor began to feign yelling at a fellow actor
where the character loses his temper with his friend over
a dispute. He was yelling very loud conveying his anger
as he yelled he stopped mid yell and began to feel drained
physically and mentally. He began to fall backward the
audience thought it was part of the play he says, "Holy
Shit!" Afterwards he fell completely on his back.

Unbeknownst to the audience he had died.
Another actor walked over in disbelief that he took
attention off the other actors by falling backward
and faking passing out for dramatic effect.
He quickly kicked the actor and bent
over telling him to get up now.
As he saw the actor not moving, he motioned
for the stage hand to close the curtain.

After cutting the performance short the other actors
felt bad the actor died while performing. After the
ambulance showed up to take the corpse of the
actor away, we showed up in front of the spirit of
the actor who was in shock to see me and Jasay.

He asked me, "So Death it is my final curtain call isn't it?"

I answer him, "Yes, fool you are dead
and will be lead into the afterlife."
Jasay tells him jokingly, "You wanted to be in
character and died on stage to show professionalism,
aren't you the consummate actor good sir?"

Not amused by this token observation
looked mortified by Jasay's question.
So I opened the portal and the Danse Macabre music
played which made the actor dance uncontrollably
and he went into the portal as I followed him.
Jasay waited for my return as he done since we
started this adventure to see what I do everyday.

When I returned, Jasay had smiled and we
went to another place so in turn for me to
take a fools soul into the afterlife.

John Omar Larnell Adams

A man, who was checking out a house, sees a rat
and gets bitten by it. He didn't realize the rat had
been genetically altered by scientist and escaped an
experimental laboratory specializing in study, research
and test of old and new diseases, viruses and plagues.

This rat had a super advanced version of
the bubonic plague in its system.

As the bite got worse soon after he was bitten.
The man made it home and was sweating. He
felt hot and started getting wounds on himself.
He remembered seeing in book as boy on the
Black Death in Europe during the Dark Ages and
recognized what was going on with him now.

He soon watched the news where the newscaster
said on TV, "Be on the lookout for a specific rat
who escaped an experimental laboratory has an
advanced version of the Bubonic Plague which
quickly begins to kill you if bitten by it."
The guy who had overheard this felt
intense dread that his end was near.

The plague spread faster making him sicker, he felt life
draining from him. His life began to flash before his
eyes and after it stopped flashing he began to die in
extreme pain. Once he did die his body lay there lifeless.
His spirit was looking at his body, Jasay and I stood at
his door, I had told Jasay to stay back because of the
advanced Bubonic plague which could be airborne.

Jasay joked with his spirit who was spooked at seeing
the two of us, "So you wanted to see what the rat
was doing and got bit had the Black Death and died,
sucks to be you eh sir?" The guy was not amused
and said to Jasay, "You little asshole I am dead!"
So to make him feel either worse or better and played
the Danse Macabre musical piece after opening
the portal so he could dance his silly ass into it.

He danced forcefully and was having a look of
terror on his face as he danced without trying
to and was doing it so uncontrollably.

After he went inside I had followed after him,
Jasay waited for me. As soon the moment I
arrived back he was ready to go again. We left to
go find more unfortunate losers who died.

While exercising a couple has the most "off the
wall" thing which happens at the gym.
While on a treadmill a wife and mother of 2
adult children walks on the rise program of
the treadmill, she then makes it speed up.
While her husband is on the pedal low bike exercise
machine and he puts the program on half speed and
programs it to go faster as he progresses in the exercise set.

As the speed goes up for both of their exercise
programs they don't realize the folly of what
was going to happen befalling this couple.
At the limit of the speed of these exercise programs
the sheer terror began for the couple.
As the speed reached its apex on the treadmill his wife
had begun to feel extreme fatigue and was thrown
from the treadmill where she landed hard breaking and
shattering her arms, legs, shins; ribs, back and head
pushing through her skin puncturing her lungs, heart,
brain, stomach; and muscles with other organs with blood
pouring out of her nose, head, mouth and ears. The sight
appalled, sickened and shocked everyone in the gym.

Her husband was hurt and disturbed by the
sudden, gruesome and quick death of his wife.
He felt pain as the apparatus inside the pedal bike stalled
and got very stuck, he pushed even though he was dead
tired. Soon the apparatus broke and impaled the husband
in the chest and pushed out his heart from his chest.
He was killed instantly, and looked with a look of
sheer terror, shock and horror from his own death.

The other gym patrons exercising got away from the morbid and sick scene of these dead people. Some called the ambulance to get rid of the dead bodies. Their spirits appeared before us, Jasay said, "So exercise builds a body, yet it tears muscles to make new muscles and yet here you are dead overexerting yourselves!"

They were offended by Jasay's comment, yet I laughed really hard though. I told him, "Take easy on the so called "fit people" Jasay."
We laughed even harder at them.

I couldn't take anymore of them both. I would look at their dead bodies, which was a very grisly and horrible scene of murder or death by accident or even on purpose, even Jasay couldn't stop laughing at them for their sheer stupidity.

While we were still laughing at them, I just opened the portal and made this stupid ass couple dance to the Danse Macabre classical piece, they went in forced to dance by the music. As they went in I couldn't stop laughing after I followed them into the portal.

Jasay couldn't stop laughing at their death scene and the people in the gym wondered why he would laugh at something so horrible. When I appeared the thing is I shocked the people inside the gym by the sight of me thinking they were next to die. We laughed looking at their dead bodies again then we disappeared to another place in search of more foolish dead people.

Jasay & I see one last thing for my day
hanging with him which is…..
We flew to the border of Israel and Palestine.
While flying in the air we see Israelis and Palestinians
fighting over their territory for the so called countries.
Jasay says to me, "This won't end well good friend."

As he said that, the foolish Middle Eastern mortals blew
each other up to shit and fired machine gun and assault
rifles into each other. Their bullet riddled bodies hit the
desert ground and burned in the heat of desert sunlight.
Just like that soon as one row of bullets hit both sides
of the warring stupid mortals over territory again.

The last two soldiers of both countries
hit the ground dying instantly.
As me and Jasay flew down to the ground to
survey the death, carnage, prejudice and stupidity
of these foolish mortals we shook our heads of the
stupid shit these mortals do and end up dead.
Their spirits came out of their bodies, Jasay said to
them, "So territory is worth killing each other over and
over again just because you can't let people live huh?"
They called him bigoted and racist in English.
They began to talk it over to me so I could
give them more time to think why they all
died so stupidly and over nothing.

I explained to them, "I don't care who is anti-Semitic,
anti-Black, anti-White; anti-Latino, anti-Asian,
anti-Middle Eastern or anti-Native Peoples of the
Americas, anti-Women, anti-Men; anti-Elderly people,

anti-Children, anti-Homosexual, Anti-Transsexual
or Transgender, or anti-Bisexual; or anti-Bestiality
participant; or whatever stupid ass hang up you dumbass
mortals say who or whatever someone is to justify you
like them or what they say about you. I am Death you
get led into the afterlife by me, fuck your principles and
you fuckers are now dead get ready for your eternity!"

With that I opened the portal and played Danse
Macabre to make these humans who always
have excuses for everything even when they die
to go over to the afterlife where they will be
tortured or live peacefully in the afterlife.

They danced and I followed after them, Jasay nodded
at me where I nodded back at him back. The Israelites
and Palestinians danced uncontrollably and forcefully
to the music while going into the portal. It closed
and Jasay waited for me this last time. I appeared
again moments later, I told him, "Now that my day
is up, how about I take you home good buddy?"

He nodded and we flew off to where he lived now.

After dropping Jasay off where he lived amongst the humans. I bid him adieu. Just not before telling him not to die or get killed. It's because the humans of Earth would have hell to pay if somehow my best friend Jasay were to die anyway or anyhow. He asks me, "Hey good buddy, who wrote the Danse Macabre classical piece you play to lead poor wretched, corrupted, unfortunate souls into the afterlife?"

I answer him, "The composer Camille Saint-Saenz wrote the music." He says, "It was a great instrumental track even its sound makes it anticlimactic for the dead though." I laugh at my best friend's suggestion and tell him, "Only you would see the funny irony in my job and the deaths of these entire silly mortals good friend!" He goes into his home and I go through the portal to see my friend from afar and await our next adventure.

Now thank you for listening to my tale.
You have witnessed A Day in the Life of Death.

The End

A FOREST FULL OF WEREWOLVES

We planned out our documentary to film a famous forest in France. We hoped to spread further how beautiful forestry and the woods can be. Even though the forest it can be dangerous as well to anyone animals included. This is including all of the animals, plants and terrain of the forest.

My friends and I gathered our money, equipment, and resources. As we planned out our schedule for filming, there was the organizing to who would film, control the microphone and who would guide everyone while reading the map.

By the way my name is Sherman Cart. My other two friends are Barbara Valley and Johnson Rock. We are environmental activists who want to do all we can to save and protect the earth from further human involvement and damages.

We had planned an overview on what to do. The plan was to have a mission plan and checklist. Barbara handled the mission plan, while Johnson handled the checklist. I went over our budget plan and shooting schedule for everyday. Also I made contact with some of France's film board to get permission to film in the set of woods we would be filming in for the five days.

The employee from the film board warned me in this manner, "Monsieur, I have to warn you that there have been werewolf sightings in that forest." He adds, "Also it is dangerous from the wildlife and if it storms you may also be in danger sir." I tried to assure the employee stating, "We know of the danger there and would like to still go and also we are on a mission to show the beauty of the earth to everyone and to protect it." I added, "Also we will be fine despite the danger."

The employee answered, "Right sir, even though there is plenty of danger even though you think that everything will be in "tip top" shape you will be fine." He adds, "Please sir, have a rain check on this happening and plan for this when it's safe, please sir?" I further explained to him, "I will press forward with my friends for this film." Begrudgingly the film board employee caved and told me, "Good luck on your endeavor sir." He hung up and I then hung up.

After I had finished speaking with the employee from the France Film Board, I told my two friends about the dangers the employee spoke of. The two of them declared, "Sherman maybe we shouldn't go through with it if werewolves, wild animals and unpredictable terrain abound the area."

I shocked by all the fear from my friends and the employee said to them, "Don't be afraid because a French person told me about the danger." I added, "Hasn't mankind courted danger in discovery of something new?" Barbara and Johnson answered, "Yes, Sherman man has seen many dangers, faced the risks and made inlands to everything newly discovered."

Both of them stated to me after their last statement, "If we die there, we will haunt you in your hospital bed and throughout the rest of your life until you die." They added, "When you become a ghost yourself we will kick your ass for the rest of eternity Sherman!" At the prospect of that I shivered in fear and nervously stated, "Right I understand and the same goes for you two if I die first." It was settled we made sure to pay our bills and pay our life insurance.

Once we gathered our equipment, we had put the rest
of our plan to film in France on the follow through.

We put our shooting schedule in our folder
of things for the documentary.
Also in it we put the storyboards, location planner.
Lastly we gathered our passports and clothing to
wear for the next couple of days as we had planned
to be in France for a week or two filming one
week and enjoying the country of France and its
sights and sounds, lastly the food and wine.

The last day of us fully in America had come upon us and
we ate with our parents separately at their homes. Once
we got settled hugged and kissed our parents goodbye, we
had decided to call each other separately to make sure that
all of us would meet one another at the airport tomorrow.

After getting back to our homes we all video chatted
each other and then said goodnight to each other and
went to sleep after clicking off our desktop computers.
The next day arrived just like that we all met up
at the airport Portland, Oregon's main airport.

After we went through boarding and put insurance on our equipment, we got on our plane to go over into France.

We had taken our seats to fly we had a stop in Denver then unto New York and La Guardia airport.
We sat in Economy seats to save money and we were given sandwich cookies and soda on the flights over. Over in New York City at La Guardia we had some Burger King, grabbed double Whopper meals with large sodas and fries. We lastly had Hershey pies and Otis Spunk Meyer cookies for dessert.

After finishing our meals we had been stuffed and waited at our gate for our flight to France.
Once the stewardess said our flight would leave in 30 minutes we got our boarding passes and passports out to board the plane.
We got on and sat near each other. Then after we got settled the three of us began reading our French language books to be able that we could communicate with the French people once we landed.

After 8 hours on the flight we landed in Paris and the pilot spoke French to us all telling us we had landed in Paris.

We got off saw most of the signs in the airport were in French. We had already exchanged our money into French Francs to spend in France whenever we needed to. Then we got to the baggage claim and grabbed our cameras and luggage, we began to get on a shuttle so we could reach the car rental place which was AVIS.

After getting our rental car we drove in the direction of our guide in France's house. Barbara called him and told him we were on our way. Johnson used the GPS on his phone with Google Maps to the GPS already in the car.

After a few back roads and turns here and there we had made it to our guide's home.

After arriving at our guide's home, we were
greeted by his daughter her name was Lynette.
She helped us and led everyone into his home.

He greeted us with the usual French greeting,
"Bonjour Monsieur's and Mademoiselle!"
We answer him, "Bonjour mon ami!"
He then asks us in English, "How was the
flight coming into France friends?"

We answer him, "It was great and no
turbulence at all mon ami."
He nods and says, "I will take you into the
woods tomorrow early so you all can film
your documentary of the forest."

We all smile and clap saying, "Great we look
forward to our filming of this beautiful forest."
His daughter says, "It is great you are filming
beware of the werewolves in the forest friends!"

Aware of the danger we faced, all of us said, "We will
be fine as long the matter is we keep living nothing will
happen as long we think positive and hope for the best."
Lynette shakes her head and says, "Right hoping for the
best sometimes works out let's hope it does friends."

We all went to sleep at our guide's home then
woke very early in the morning at 330am.
The three of us took separate showers, after
dressing and putting lotion on ourselves,
we put our clothes and deodorant on.

159

We brushed our hair as well. Lynette made us croissants and sausage with eggs and red wine. Afterwards we put our equipment back into the car then our guide got into his car and drove as we drove behind him on our way to the forest to film our documentary finally.

The minute we arrived in the woods and set
everything up, we knew we were golden.

We set up our camera and the microphones to
record Barbara or Johnson guiding us through the
woods detailing and describing the beautiful forest
we would occupy for the next couple of days.
Then we set up our tents to stay in while
we are in this beautiful forest.
We had looked over our shooting schedule. Our
guide bid us all adieu and good luck, lastly to
watch out for werewolves here in the forest.

As soon the matter of filming started we began to
find our rhythm and proceeded accordingly.

The first day of shooting "went off
without a hitch" as they say.
We had filmed the trees as Barbara spouted word after
word about the forest and its humble beginnings.
As she kept on we took up filming as I held the
camera steady and followed closely to her.

Johnson would guide her with cue cards on his
left and when she had to stop so she could avoid
hitting her head or bumping or even falling over
onto or into a tree or hole in the forest.
While filming we saw some locals of the forest we
stopped and asked them questions varying about
the forest and more of its scenery. They would
answer accordingly to our questions answering
very detailed and in French and English.

They told us in English, "Once you're done filming
for the day come by there the local man and his
supposed girlfriend or wife pointed in the direction
of where they wanted us to meet them for some
desserts and wine after we finished today."

We said on film to them, "Sure we will stop by there
after we are done filming for today good sir!"
The rest of filming went on and we had finished our first
day of shooting as the dark and starry night came upon us.

Once filming the first day was done, we met
up with the locals we met while shooting.

As we sat with them at their campfire, they
handed us all croissants covered in butter
with stuffing of jam inside of it.
They asked us if we were Americans. We answered
them, "Yes good people we are all three Americans."
They smiled as they said, "We rarely get Americans in
our woods." They added, "Also we will be as cooperative
and kind to you all as the three of you have been to us
since arriving in our forest to film your documentary."
We had smiled and said, "We are very much so
enjoying our stay in France so far and hope to finish
filming our documentary so we can show the world
our planet is beautiful and needs to be protected by
everyone on Earth as well because it is our home."

Once we finished our statements we just smiled and
laughed at each others stories of all our childhoods.

The night dragged on as we ate croissants and drank wine with our new local French people. They were the one who we met earlier during filming the first day.

While smiling they took us over to where they all lived in a nice size house where they all resided in the forest.

We were all amazed at how nice the house looked and felt better. Then my friend Johnson asked, "How long have you all been living in this house?" The elderly gentleman and woman exclaimed in English, "We have been here since the 1920s." The thought of all this amazed us.

After we finished eating the croissants and wine, the three of us bid the new friends good night and went back to our tents to sleep. It seemed comfy and we all fell fast asleep from the wine.

During the second day of filming, something
changed during the evening while getting our
last shots or dailies for our shoot. I saw while
looking through the camera lens a large humanoid
wolf or werewolf, if that's what I really saw.

It made me feel uneasy.

So I asked Johnson and Barbara after we finished for the
day, and showed them the footage I took of the werewolf.
They were shocked and more than a little bit frightened
by the sight of a werewolf in the mid-evening.

Barbara said to me and Johnson, "Maybe we should cut
our time filming short and get the hell out of here!"
Johnson agreed with her saying, "Sherman man,
we might want to get out while we can."
I had thought of it and said, "If one appears and we all
get a glimpse of it then we can leave alright my friends."

Our new friends appeared again with
Danishes, pastries and milk this time.

That night while eating Danishes and pastries with our
French friends, I asked if there were any werewolves
ever spotted in the area. It got quiet then and there
at the campfire. They gave me the details of the
legend of werewolves in the very forest we were in.

The elder patriarch of the family stated, "Long
ago in this forest werewolves appeared in this
forest, which were interpreted by writers of fiction
as werewolf fiction. It may be stated they appear
during full moons. Also they can attack people in
forest or in rural, and suburban, lastly urban areas
or even have sex with human men and women."

"Scared out of her shit", soon Barbara asks,
"Is that really true Renoir' sir?"
He answers, "Yes Mademoiselle, it is true." He
adds, "That story has been told to me as my father
and grandfather and many paternal ancestors
have told each other for many centuries."
He lastly states, "None will bother you as long as
they don't smell your natural pheromones."

Barbara then lets out a quick sigh of relief and says,
"That is a relief if I ever heard one." She lastly says
to Johnson and me, "Let's get a move on to our
tents and don't get horny you two numb nuts!"

So with that we bid adieu to our friends. Johnson
winked at the daughter of the middle aged

man and woman of the French friends who
lived in the house nestled in these woods.
Barbara and I shrugged and asked each other,
"He won't listen to anybody for shit will he?"

We then made our way unto the tents we slept in.

John Omar Larnell Adams

That night I heard my friends fornicating with some of
our new friends. For some reason or another as I went
to sleep, I overheard the statement of "OH Shit!"
As I awoke the next morning my friend Johnson came
into my tent. He was distraught and terrified.

He then asked me, "Hey Sherman, I think I was
attacked by one of the werewolves last night a
female one take a look at this would you?"
I mocked him saying the same thing in his voice tone.
I told him, "I'll look, let's see it shall we?"

I lifted his shirt and saw claw marks on his rib
cage. I was now scared and yelled, "AHH!!"
Barbara came into my tent to see what happened,
she asked while yawning, "Sherman why are
you screaming so much this morning huh?"
I told her, "Bar look at this shit would you?"

She glimpsed at the claw marks and said, "Holy
shit that's gross!" She asked Johnson,
Did a bear attack you last night idiot leaving
pieces of pastry or Danishes in here?'
Johnson answers with some terror in his voice,
"No a female werewolf fucked me last night and
scratched me to all in the former night."

Barbara said, "Sure it did, we are awaiting a werewolf to
be seen by all of us to be able that we all could leave here."

She adds, "Let's just get our shit together and
we'll do some more filming if not we'll take
you to a hospital or doctor alright?"

We put a change of clothes on and
decided to film anyway.

After going through our third day of filming,
we had to shut down early that day to take our
friend Johnson to a local hospital. So that he
could be checked out from his animal attack scars
which he said came from a female werewolf.
As we got into the car, my friend winced
even though we put anti septic and peroxide
on the wound to avoid infection.

Between his whining and pain from his wounds,
Barbara and I discussed whether or not we should
continue filming our documentary or not.
As we kept going past the forest, the GPS led us all
into the nearby town where the hospital was.
Once we pulled into its parking lot we
stopped and parked in a parking space.

Then we helped Johnson as we led him into
the emergency room, he whined and moaned
from the pain of his animal scar wounds.
Soon as we waited, a doctor who spoke English
showed up and took our friend into the back and
we waited for the doctor to administer some more
first aid and whatever else could help Johnson.

Some hours went by and we saw Johnson who walked
out and showed us his wound bandaged. The doctor
told us to try and let him rest so his wounds would
heal, also telling us to not have him do any heavy
lifting or he would open his wounds completely up.

We along with Johnson gave some Francs to pay for his emergency room usage to deal with the wounds.

We then waved goodbye and thanked the doctor for his help, and we left the hospital's emergency room, lastly drove off back to the forest so we could finish our documentary.

After he was checked out and had his wound cleaned. We settled down for the night. Our friends didn't come by that night. As I tried to go back into sleep again, I overheard this, "OH Fuck Me!"

I thought my two friends were fornicating together. So I thought he was an idiot for trying to reopen his wounds.

I went to sleep that night and tried to ignore the fools for trying to open his wounds fucking with someone else.

The next day came, I awoken to my other friend
Barbara opening my tent and she said, "I had a
male werewolf fucking me the other night!"

I sardonically mocked her and said, "I had a
male werewolf fucking me the other night.
That line which was repeated by me.

Annoyed she went and then took herself to storming off
away from me. We went on with the fourth day of filming.
The day went well and we were moving along smoothly,
strangely Johnson's wound healed completely.

Once the day of shooting completed we decided
to "turn in early" that night and sleep.
So we did as we felt a bit drowsy from yesterday's
happenings and the waiting in the emergency room.

That night my friend Johnson had started
yelling, Barbara and me watched as he
turned into a werewolf before our eyes.

He began to go into the other direction. We
followed him and hid between some trees.

He went to the home of our new French friends
who made wait outside. They came out and under
the moon they became werewolves as well.

We were now shocked at this happening, we
saw them howl while looking at the moon.
The rest of our friends that were now werewolves
began fucking each other including the daughter
who I know found out she was the female werewolf
who scratched Johnson while fucking him.

Barbara and I continued watching from a distance
in the bushes. This odd animal fucking went on for
some of the night. As they all went into the French
friend's home for some kind of werewolf orgy, me
and Barbara watched mortified at this sight.

After some time they all stopped tired and
exhausted from their intense sex group session.
We turned around from the bushes and
decided to sneak back to our tents.

The night was starting to fade as me and my other friend Barbara went back to our tents before dawn.

I went to sleep fast and was still shocked from seeing my friend and new friends turning into werewolves. As I awoke the thing is I noticed a female werewolf who had been fucking me while I slept.

I said very loudly, "Holy Fuck!" I orgasm med and shook from the intense orgasm. My friend Barbara came to my tent so she could see what the commotion was. She stated from the off putting bestiality sight, "Oh Shit Man!"

As I came inside the female werewolf shook hard and violently from her very own orgasm as all my semen emptied into her, she took her snatch and gripped my dick getting my seed. She turned and got off me howled at the moon and then went off in the direction of our French friend's home.

The morning had come upon us suddenly; Barbara and I had decided since last night to continue our documentary even though we felt that the two of us could finish without Johnson if we needed to.

We started the fifth day of filming, a bit
drained from the night before. We saw our
friend Johnson and he was very happy.

After he was turned back to normal by the sunlight
of early morning, we ask him while a bit angry,
"So you were in pain and moaning, also whining
like a little bitch and were turning into a werewolf,
lastly you knew it the whole time huh?
He answered, "Yes I knew it the time when our
friends came by the first day, and the middle aged
couple's daughter told me about them all."

Barbara and I told Johnson, "You're an asshole
man making us worry about you and think
you were turning rabid with rabies."
Sarcastically he answers, "I am an asshole huh?"
He adds, "Are the ass cheeks covered in sweat
and dirt which I am encased in too?"
Both us tell him, "Fuck you Johnson you dipshit!"

We all stopped our squabbling and went back to
our objective of filming the documentary.
The day was going very well as Barbara continued
narrating and leading us through some more of the forest.

The days flew by and we were nearly done filming.
We had begun to include the French friends turning
into werewolves. It seemed our forest documentary
had become more of a horror comedy film.

We were still uneasy about filming people
who were really werewolves.
So we soldiered on filming and even interviewing
them about their lives and how they live with all
the other wildlife and nature of the forest.

They all replied, "Happily and fully in tune
with all the life throughout this forest," they
said happily to us while we filmed them.

After our last day of filming, Barbara and as did myself go out and confronted our French friends on being werewolves. They didn't deny it. They told us to embrace them and our friend for their uniqueness.

We swallowed our pride and asked if they were sure we could us the footage of them turning to werewolves and lastly if they felt their safety would be compromised if we let the world see this documentary. They answered us, "We have no fear of tomorrow and if we are captured and experimented on because of mans curiosity of the unknown or supernatural so be it." They then added, "We are happy with our lives and for meeting you all who have become our friends in the long run."

After hearing this we concluded our film. Barbara and I talked it over and decided we were done with our documentary.

Our friend, Johnson had decided to stay behind and live with the French forest werewolf clan. Which caused me and Barbara to look unconcerned in his situation; we shrugged in our indifference to him and them.

We had left him there and not before wishing him great luck and success with his life in the French forest with his new love and family or soon to be in laws.

After gathering the camera and equipment we mad our way back to our guide's home. He welcomed us both back and we told him what happened to our friend Johnson. Which he said, "C'est la vie!" So we left the next morning earlier got to our gate at Paris's airport and boarded our plane then left to go back over into America for return trip back home.

We made our way back to America and edited
our film with an added touch of a film score.
Also we did some ADR for the voice over with
Barbara leading viewers into our world detailing the
beautiful forest in France we wanted to present our
fellow Earthlings so they could help fix the planet
and make things better for future generations.

Now Barbara and I looked forward to the future after
we did the final post production for the documentary.

Barbara and I had developed an intimate relationship. Later we were married and had children. We keep in touch with our friend who took up residence in France. I later had discovered that I had a hybrid kid with the female werewolf who snuck into my tent.

The one thing still that is in my memory:

I remember when I was in ***A Forest Full of Werewolves***.

The End

THE VAMPIRE'S HOME

The country that I come from is Germany.
Sure we descend from Norwegians. We have like
every country or continent, a history of good, bad
and ugly times. If you have read a history book
on Ancient, Classic or Modern Germany then
I don't need to tell you of anything then.

My name is Handel Bier, a young adult Caucasian
German male. There are many good and great
times in my life from what I have surmised from
everything in my life so far. I grew up in Berlin
after the post tearing down of the Berlin Wall.

My early life was warm, loving and encouraging. My
father or Dad was Heinrich Bier, my mother Gwendolyn
Bier. I also have a younger sister Wilhelmina. As we
got older my sister turned her musical tastes onto
German Dance music, with American Dance music
and American Rap and Hip Hop. My music palette
became Rock Music, Jazz and classical music.

My parents had us take up music lessons. My instruments
were piano and guitar. My sister took up bass and drums.

After growing up my sister and I went our separate ways.
Soon I had found a job being an accountant for a
large national Brokerage firm nestled in Germany.
Well after college and getting an internship at the firm I
work at now. It seems things have worked out very well.

I call clients to check on them and if they need
me to fill out paperwork for their finances and
also do their taxes. I have many high class and
wealthy clients throughout Germany.
There are the Dussell family, and the Schneider family,
lastly the Hulf family I particularly deal with.

All of them are warm and welcoming people. They have
such kind words to say, and I reply polite and kind words
to them as well. As their esteemed families have dealt
with the firm for many generations, I must keep up with
all their affairs accordingly well financially anyway.

Most of all I live a bachelor's life, mainly consisting
of many women who venture into my bed.
So many times I almost forget the names
of these women I lay on a daily basis.
I am not a gigolo by anybody's standards and you
can call me a male slut if it helps your situation.

My job as an accountant is a very profitable one.
A lot of times I incur tips and extra pay from
the three families I mentioned earlier.
I drive a two seat Mercedes Benz in the A class. My home
is very quaint or medium sized if you will say it is.

I have a backyard and sometimes I have
a beer or Jagermeister on my back porch
whenever the moment hits me.
My life could get no better. The thing is, I have
a great job that pays well, my pension is steadily
increasing, an excess of women at my beck and call.

My car is nice and drives, as well
performs well on the Autobahn.
What more could a man ask for, well….
How about more work to keep myself occupied.

I should have remembered the saying,
"Be careful what you wish for."
How I sometime dread or grow optimistic
over this decision of more work.

After going over some accounts, I discovered
a discrepancy with one of our clients.
The client was Count Brahms Strauss.
After going through some of his file I had seen
that he lived in a castle outside of Berlin.
He lived alone and with his butler and maid, he was
born in the 1910s, the strange thing was he looked like
he was 20 or 30 years old and not like a very old man.

This bothered me. He had outstanding assets
in his name throughout Germany.
I seen he had at least a hundred or more
checking and savings accounts in each city
or town throughout the country.

It just made no since that a man with all this cash
distributed all over Germany could not know
about it. Someone maybe his butler and maid
had not made him aware of his vast fortune.

The matter made me call my boss Ralf Handel to see
about the matter and call the count on this matter.

My boss called me in and had a short discussion
over this client I found in our records.
He asked me, "So Handel, you found something
amiss with the Strauss account did you?"
I answered him, "Yes Mr. Handel it seems Mr. Strauss
did not know about his accounts throughout Düsseldorf
sir." I added, "Can I please call him and arrange a
meeting with him at his home if I could sir?"

Mr. Handel tapped the bottom of his chin and said
to me, "I will inform you when your assignment
to Count Strauss's home will commence."
He then asked me, "Are you sure that you yourself are up
to this task, and will accept the outcome if necessary?"
I told him, "If I can help the count in any way that
I will do for him, so be it and that in any shape or
form my job will satisfactory and efficient sir."

Mr. Handel said with a smile which made me
somewhat uneasy, "Good Handel my boy, I will call
you back into my office to take the assignment as soon
the layout of your work pervades the workload."
With that I left his office with anticipation at my desk
for the outcome of my find and new assignment.

Just like that Mr. Handel came out and gave me my
new file and with it the details of my assignment and
lastly he had called Mr. Strauss's home to inform the
butler and maid of soon to be presence at the castle.

Shortly after my boss gave me my assignment, I went and
made my way toward our client's castle outside of Berlin.
The drive was said to be 45 minutes
to the castle west of the city.
As I drove the lights had begun to start signaling nightfall.

The highway led me to the onset of suburbia and
after the rural countryside soon took hold.
My thoughts were, "It is only for a couple of
days what is the worst could happen to me?"
Little did I know that the things which would be seen
there would cause me to tell a story like this one to
you the happy and enthusiastic reader of this story.

Once I made the drive there, I met his lawyer,
publicity agent, stylist and his family member.
They greeted me by saying, "Guttentag Mr. Bier!"
I replied the same hello saying they told me in German.

We had all greeted each other and hugged, lastly
shook hands. Then we all went into our vehicles and
retrieved our bags which had our clothes to stay for the
temporary time we were staying at the Count's castle.

His lawyer's name was Johann Rottweiler, his publicity
agent was Heidi Moltz, his stylist was Susan Rult; and
his family member was his female cousin Gretel Strauss.

She greeted me and lastly hugged me.
I thought that maybe the stay at the
castle won't be so bad after all.

The butler and his maid came out of the castle
and made their way toward all of us.
They said to everyone, "Guttentag everyone!"
They then gestured to take our bags into the castle
which we all handed them all of our bags they
took them all and left them at the front door's
opening hallway inside the lobby of the castle.

After his butler and maid showed us in we
looked around this big and lush castle.
We saw the hugeness and grandeur
splendor of this huge castle.
There was very little hints of femininity, such as
roses and tulips scaled and set in vases leading
to the stair way where we would be staying and
sleeping at as told to us by the butler and maid.

The masculine touches were as seen, marble
floors and pictures of death in war shown in
paintings, also nude women in statue form.
It was like a big male mind tease to anyone
who was all to see this sight of this large and
uncommon home in this modern age.
Even though castles all still are a sight to see as
long they were in different parts of the world.

After getting settled into our rooms the maid
went and told me and the Count's lawyer
and everyone else to all meet at the stairwell.

The butler had gathered the stylist, publicist and
female relative of the Count to meet there too.

The butler and maid began to yell, "Madam come
meet our guests of the Count at the castle."

I saw a woman after "madam" was called. The thing
that shocked me more than anything the woman
of the castle was my younger sister Wilhelmina.
I had the look like of someone showed me a graphic
sex scene in a pornographic film for the first time
as if seeing sex for the first time in front of me.

If only you seen my adult entertainment "virginal eyes"
look on my face you would probably laugh at me.

The butler and maid introduced her to everyone
as soon Wilhelmina went to shake my hand,
I said to her, "Greetings baby sister."
She swallowed and said to me, "Hello big brother!"
Everyone looked shocked that we were brother and sister.

We had a quick hug. Then we discussed
the matter of me being at the castle.
Once we got almost caught up, the Count
came downstairs to greet us all. He said,
"Guttentag and good evening everyone!"

We all greeted him as well.
He asked, "Let's all have dinner together alright?"
We nodded. He then asked the butler and maid if the
dinner was ready. The two of them nodded at him.
They then lead us into the dining room to eat.

It was full of bratwurst, sauerkraut, potatoes
and broccoli. Also they served red wine.

We all had dinner that night in a large dining room. We had discussed many things. I took this chance to talk to my sister during this meal. I asked her, "When did you decide to be a rich count's lover?"

She answered me, "Well brother, I met him at a club and he swept me off my feet, we then had a few dates; lastly he asked me to live with him the fact of the matter which I did and here we are." I made an hmm sound. Then I told the Count, "I wonder what kind of lady as my sister is made him want her so bad for?" He answered me, "Mr. Bier, I saw her on the dancefloor and decided I had to be with her and after taking her out to dinner more than a few times she wanted to live with me after I asked her.

The two of them convinced me. The publicist told the count of future meetings with the elite wealthy families throughout Germany to discuss further endeavors to expand their fortunes outside of Germany. The stylist told him that she had picked out different outfits or well tailored clothes to use at these meetings to wear and look sophisticated and masculine and handsome.

The lawyer convinced him to talk it over with me about his accounts throughout Germany and to see about his other properties and pay taxes on them.

Then we all finished our meal and wine.
We all dispersed separately and went to our rooms.
I had realized after the dinner that my room was
very close to the Count and my sister's room.

Once dinner was done, I went to my room to change
in pajamas. Then the thought which occurred to
me was the well being of my younger sister.
I had gotten ready to get some sleep for the night.
Just then I had heard some laughing
or giggling for some reason.

The thought of or maybe it was curiosity that
compelled me to go see what my sister really saw in
this old man who was mysteriously young looking.
I decided to go see their intimacy first hand and witness
what had made my sister be in love with the Count.
So I crept out of my room and left my door part way
open to let myself out while giving off the illusion that I
am still in bed either sleeping or getting ready to sleep.

After making my way down to the entrance of the door
leading into the Count and my sister's room, I decided
to secretly look inside to see what was so damn funny.
The sight that I would see gives me shivers
to this day even though it showed my sister
had become a full fledged woman.

My sister was nude. She had mounted the Count and she
was riding him in the cowgirl sex position. He was on
the bottom pumping and thrusting inside of her, he was
also moaning, she was panting. I watched them fucking
each other for a good while, and also the sex funk was
starting to waif outside the door into the hallway.

The smell was a bit overpowering, I had to take
it a guy "having his way" with my sister.

After they stopped the smell seemed to
surge even more after they finished.
I moved away to my room again. I heard my sister tell
the Count she was tired and she would go to sleep now.

The Count had put a robe on, he told my sister,
"Honey you get some rest, I will go downstairs
to get some milk or water so I could sleep."
My sister cut the light out and fast went to sleep.

After seeing my sister fucking this rich man who had
owned the castle, it had occurred to me and I thought my
sister was under a sexual spell or some sort of sex magic.
Just the thought of seeing them fucking made
me unnerved and slightly nauseous.
"OH Shit!" I had thought. My sister is being dick
drunk from an old man with a pure baby face.

Then I smacked myself a little bit hard.
It seemed that staying here in the castle wasn't bad, just
hard to take even though my sister was a grown woman
it is hard to see your sister fucking someone. Even
though you have known each other all your lives we
keep our sex lives completely hidden from each other.

The Count had made his way downstairs
from what I overheard.
I had decided to follow and see him drinking this water
or milk to make sure he really was going to do just that.

I began to follow after the rich count. Then while
following him, I saw something frightening.
As I followed him he went into the basement of his
home, a sparse or even slight light was illuminating
the steps leading into the basement below.

Once slightly down there, I heard Beethoven's Sixth
Symphony playing, some women lined up and tied to rope
in the ceiling smiled sexually and deviantly at the Count.
It seemed the perversion and sexual deviance
just doesn't stop with this guy.

I saw him rip the clothing off all these women and he
kissed each of them passionately and deeply on the lips.
He backed away and let his tongue dangle out of his
mouth as each of the women's tongues went to his as well.
Both he and all of them were sucking each others tongues.

He began to perform separate instances of Cunnilingus
on the women. They began to yell, "DA!" As he
continue moving his mouth toward their clitorises
and sucked it while eating their pussies out.
Some he ate out so well the women squirted
in his mouth female ejaculate.

He then proceeded to fuck them savagely and quickly,
lastly hard. The women moaned and writhed sexually.
He kept going. Then after sometime he shook all over
and moaned as he had orgasm med inside these women.
The women squirted again. They told him, "Thank
you for stooping me Count!" They were still panting.
He then said to them, "Now you ladies get a treat."

He then told them to close their eyes, and he grew
fangs from his incisors, I realized he was a vampire like
in the movies. Except it was real life in front of me.
He then grabbed each one of the women. After
grabbing them separately he bit their necks and
they moaned as if they were having an orgasm.

Some did orgasm from this, and they began
to squirt as they died. He moved to each
one and did the same to all the rest.
The weird thing about this it made me
aroused from the deviance and sexual nature
of this event going down in front of me.

The butler untied the women. I left as soon the last
woman died. I crept back to my room upstairs, I was
still scared and aroused from what I seen this night.
I felt that as soon my sister woke tomorrow I would
pull her to the side and tell her about her lover.

After telling my sister she was "stooping" a
vampire. She shrugged it off as nonsense.
My sister was thought that I was becoming "stir crazy"
from staying in the castle and not going out to the garden
outside or walking around the castle grounds on my own.
I assured her that I was not going crazy
from being cooped up in the castle.

Lastly I tried to convince her that I was telling the truth.
The thing is I told her to sleep with the
Count if they did that kind of thing.
Fake sleeping and follow behind me to see what
happens whenever everyone else is asleep.

She told me that, "I am leaning on
following you to see if this is true."

One day, I asked her to follow me as I crept
secretly and stealthily behind the count. She
begrudgingly went with me. She had sex with
the Count and reeked of sex and semen.

We waited for the Count to go downstairs and
do his business with some new women like what
I saw the night, which was two nights ago.
As he went downstairs, we were close behind him.

My sister saw the women he had tied up by
the butler. This time the maid had told the
women along with the butler they were there
as a reverse harem orgy for the Count.
They all said, "YA!"
He proceeded to kissing them deeply and
passionately on the lips with tongue too. They
then began to suck each others tongues.
Then he would pull away from them, and
began ripping off their clothes.

He then began fucking these women savagely, hard,
and quickly. Making them all moan and writhe and
ride his dick while standing and being tied up. All of
them squirted female ejaculate. My sister was appalled
and shocked by these actions, mad because she thought
he was her only one she loved and made love to.

He then told these new women to close their
eyes. He grew long incisors and became a full
on vampire. He bit them and they moaned and
writhed, to me and my sister's surprise some of

them began grinding in place as he bit them. Before dieing they moaned louder and squirted again.

My sister had enough and decided to
go back upstairs with me.
She told me, "That was completely shocking
and appalling, yet I was deeply aroused
sexually by it older brother."

I walked away from my sister "in the same
boat", so to speak from what we saw this night.
I went to sleep and so did my sister.

After seeing the horror of him drinking other
people's blood through a bite in their neck, my
sister wanted to stop the count once and for all.
Once my sister had begun to continue the ruse
that she was still in love with the Count, we had
started to formulate a plan to take him out.
I thought of the way we should carry out these actions,
she was thinking of what to use for killing the count.

Sometime later, we had thought of getting the others
besides us, excluding the butler and maid in our scheme
or plan to kill the count and escape from the castle.
Also we were going to call the police to arrest the butler
and maid for bringing women to be killed by the count.

After revealing our plan and showing the others in the castle staying with us what the count does for sustenance. They all formulated a plan with me and my sister to take him out. Also we wanted to escape from a sudden death from the count if he found us all out.

The others were shocked at the Count's actions and deeds, including his younger female cousin, who had said, "He is a disgrace to the Brahms family as a vampire, not being human."

My sister and I began running scenarios on how we would execute our plan to do this efficiently and correctly without any mistakes at all during the plan.

We had all gotten into groups. Planning which
group should do whatever if need be to the count.

The women would gather and slowly use chloroform
on the maid. While the lawyer and I would chloroform
the butler. Then we would have the ladies open the
door of the Count, and the lawyer would give facial
expressions to me so that I would get the go ahead
to stake the Count in the heart and kill him.

While the Count would talk over ways to improve
the castle amongst themselves, we all would go
through the motions of how and doing the act of
getting to the butler and maid, lastly entering the
Count's room and staking him through the heart.

Soon after another day we had our routine of faking
or feigning politeness to the butler, maid and the
Count. While we had been keeping our intent of
getting them hidden from the three of them "playing
it off" being nice, polite and cordial to them.

The butler and maid of the castle began to
grow suspicious of me and my sister.

They wondered if we knew about the Count's
extracurricular activities at night.
My sister and I began to shrug off their
accusations saying, "No we didn't know of
the Count doing anything at night."

They thought we could be lying, so after a couple of hours
they lost their arousal of suspicion from me and my sister.
The Count had thought we had all seen him. So he began
to question me and my sister separately or together.

After convincing the count that we were not planning any
harm to him, soon afterwards he felt at ease somehow.

My sister, me and the others staying at the
castle had to "play it off" that we really were
going to give harm to the Count.
He seemed so oblivious to our acting
which was sub par at best.

My sister continued sleeping with the Count and the sex
smell still filled the hallway and lingered into the morning.
The rest of us still had to try getting used
to the constant sex funk in the air within
the hallway leading to our rooms.
We still had to soldier on with our plan.

The two of us and the others in the castle
began to speak in code to confuse the
count, the butler and lastly the maid.

As we used odd enunciations in English words
to hide what we were all talking about.
The Count, maid and butler all thought we had a
strange fascination with the English language.

We had begun to work out scenarios with the group now
to act out or walkthrough the attack on the count.
Once we began running it with a great rhythm
and poise, we decided we should take a break
from doing practice runs of our attack.

We planned the day when we would
strike against the count.

In a day or two the actions against the Count would
be acted out and we the group could all kill him.
We went through the motions one more time.
It seemed we all had it down to a science
now. There was no room for error. We had all
participants ready to handle their jobs.

It seemed time stood still as we waited for tomorrow
to come to act our attack and kill the Count.

John Omar Larnell Adams

The day came and we snuck into the maid and
butler's room and used chloroform on them to knock
them out as they awoke before from us startling
them. We then tied them up separately with rope
binding their hands, arms, legs; feet and torsos.

We had carried them to the bottom of the
steps so when they woke the authorities would
have no trouble apprehending them. The
Count was next on our "to do" list.
We moved cautiously toward the Count's room.

It all seemed to run like clockwork for all of us.
We felt better knowing the nightmare within
this castle was soon to be ending.

We soon arrived at the count's room. We had
begun in groups our attack on him.

The lawyer directed me with a hand gesture to get
ready to drive the stake into the Count's heart.

I crept so quietly and stealthily toward the Count
as he lay sleeping there in his very large bed.
Soon I got next to him from the left. Then I had
brought the stake over his chest and took a hammer,
lastly drove the stake into his heart with the
hammer. He went in a loud voice, "OH Shit!"
He squirmed and writhed in pain and
finally died right there in his bed.

The nightmare was over and now the only thing
to do was call the police to arrest the butler and
maid when they confess to their deeds gathering
and bringing women so the Count could fuck
them and kill them by biting their necks.

After the scary moments in the castle, the local police were notified. The butler and maid were brought up on kidnapping charges for all the people they brought in for the count to feed on. I remember the chilling fact of it all:

That time we spent all of our time at ___***The Vampire's Home***___ was memorable and some of us lived.

The End

WAS IT REALLY A GHOST?

There was a time when I wasn't
scared of anything as a child.
My life during this early stage in that era
was optimistic and full of hope.
The main thought I had was just to play with my
friends are James Terry a Caucasian boy, Jordan Bare an
African American boy and Tabitha Britney a Caucasian
girl. We live in Dayton, Ohio. We are all 6 years old.
There was a guy who lived in Lexington, Kentucky who
would play with us when he visited his family in Dayton
named John Omar Larnell Adams. Our neighborhood
is nice or middle class if you're trying to keep up.

There was an old man who lived in our neighborhood.
His name was Walking Bear, from what our parents told
us he is a Pawnee. Which is one of the ancient tribes of
the Native Peoples of the Americas. They were once all
over the Ohio Valley before the Valley was called that.

He is a peaceful and kind man. He calls John from
Lexington Rain Fire. John told us it's the name his
granddad in Georgia calls him because his grandpa

was Cherokee and John with his grandpa's ancestor
had the name Rain Fire and John looks exactly
like him so he gave him his ancestor's name.

Walking Bear was always friendly and cordial. He always
shows us his wife who was also Pawnee as well in old
pictures and tells us sometimes stories of their life together.

My friends and I love going to see
our neighbor on a given day.
He was always so nice and kind to all of us.
Walking Bear always had this kind of bread made by
some of the Pawnee whenever we ate it at his home.

When John from Lexington, Kentucky
would come to Dayton to visit his Uncle and
Auntie he would hang out with us.
John would tell us stories about living in Lexington and
going to the Washington, DC area as well. He would
lastly describe his life as a child actor in Hollywood and
around the world in other countries and continents.

Walking Bear would speak the Pawnee language
with him and John would speak it back to him.
They would always use the word
Kosata when talking a lot.
It seemed they were content with their conversations.

After talking with Walking Bear for a while, we would
get ready to leave his home to play outside together.
We would play Chase, a game where everyone
scatters and the person giving chase to everyone
else had to catch either one person or everyone.
It was a fun game. We all enjoyed playing
this game or hide and seek.

Our childhood seemed that it could be no better.

Another day ended after school ended for
that day and we played outside together.
We all decided to play baseball together
even Tabitha wanted to as well.
She was the pitcher, while James was the catcher. I
was at bat, while Jordan and John played outfield.

The game went by fairly quickly and then we
were all sweaty and dirty from the extended
play of playing baseball together.
I went home as the others also made their
way to the homes they lived in too.

The weekend came up and we decided to go over to
our Pawnee neighbor's home to hang out with him.
Walking Bear began to talk of his people to us and
we listened with full intent of learning more about
Pawnee history through his great and eloquent stories.
He told of villages and a great people who lived in them.
Their daily lives and what they ate. How they hunted
and gathered berries and other fruit from the forest.

Also he talked about their elder in the village who
everyone looked up to for wisdom and gave him respect.
The chief was the leader and commanded attention
from everyone, lastly gave his thoughts and
some sort of mission statement to everyone else
how they would live and somehow prosper.

He even spoke of how the pioneers and settlers interrupted
everything to the Pawnee and the other tribes within the
Ohio Valley and throughout what was left of the Native
Peoples land area throughout the rest of the country
before it was taken from them by Mexicans, Spanish,
French, and Dutch; English and American settlers.

It seemed like a happy story at first, it ended
tragically with a lot of the Native Peoples losing
their culture or being forced to mix with the
settlers who stayed with them in their villages.

John who was still Rain Fire by Walking Bear was
asked, "Rain, just how did he feel about his people being
stripped of everything and left to pick up the pieces?'

John answered, "It feels bad, if I express
how I really feel about Colonialism to
Abiyala, my friends here will hate me."

Walking Bear nodded and said, "You answered
how I thought you would Rain."
With that we left with mixed emotions on how
our country's history is dark and sad one.
John told us in Utopia books, "Successful civilizations
are boosted by the work and misery of the
downtrodden within the successful civilization."

That analogy summed up every place throughout
history including North and South America sadly.
All of this was much for our young minds and we
continued to soldier on looking for the positive in
this suburban life within America in the Midwest.

Some people in the neighborhood stated he has lived well over 150 years as the rumor said. Some were speculating that he was a ghost from an old time. Our parents were less than enthused by us all hanging out at Walking Bear's home.

They said rude, horrible, racist and bigoted things about Walking Bear which hurt our feelings and we saw where all his sad stories about his people and the troubling things from the past with the settlers who had pushed his people off their land and segregated them to reservations stemmed from and the attitudes of the settlers reborn in our parents unwarranted hate and disdain for Walking Bear made us all sick and worried about our parents, lastly making us wonder why they were call civilized in the first place.

We had thought of something which would carry on with us into adulthood. We abhorred acceptance and tolerance of others despite national or ethnic origin. Also they told us, "He may be a ghost". Which we didn't believe for any second of time we had up or went to sleep.

We never believed that dribble and
continued hanging out at his home.
The more he told of us stories of his people
made us want to help others even more and be
better people to our fellow human beings.
Walking Bear as always was very cordial and polite to us.

He gave us juice, apple and grape juice to all of us.
Also he would ask us about how school was going.
We would answer him saying, "Oh, we are doing fine in
school, participating and learning as we go Walking Bear."

He smiled and we decided to keep talking with
him learning how we could get respect and
still be admirable as an elderly person.
It was always a great day hanging
out Walking Bear's home.

We asked him whether he were a ghost or not. He would
laugh and ask, "Where we had heard such talk."
Then we told him, "The people who told
us you were a ghost was our parents."
He laughed again and asked, "You don't
believe that kind of talk do you?"

We understood the humor in his quip
about the accusation he was a ghost.
After he said that we laughed at that notion too with him.
We kept on laughing at the silly thought he was a ghost.

Soon after we finished laughing we decided
to leave Walking Bear's home and go to our
own houses. We waved to him and said,
"Goodbye Walking Bear our friend."
He waved back at us and said, "Goodbye
little friends and have a good night."

We then made our way back to our homes.

After we tried convincing the adults, that he was
no ghost. We put on a campaign to change other
people's opinions and thoughts about him.
We went from door to door throughout our
neighborhood to tell people in and within our
entire happy neighborhood he was no ghost.
Some of discussion with the adults in our
neighborhood fell on deaf ears.
We said jokingly to the adults in our neighborhood,
"It seems you all's racist and bigoted talk of Walking
Bear seems so good even though it is ignorant."
We added, "You all are great to your
fellow man aren't you?"

They were not amused by our snarky humor.
They told us, "Even though you all are children,
I have to tell you brats to fuck off now!"
We laughed at all of the adult people in our
neighborhood's discouragement with us
making light of their bigotry and racism.

We continued this journey through our neighborhood.
Even though the adults showed disdain toward us for
being great to one of the Native Peoples of the Americas.
Their downright horrible actions made us
dislike others for the first time in our lives.

Even John showed a bit of dislike toward
the adults in our neighborhood. He was
normally a happy and positive person.

Some days when we hung out at our Pawnee neighbors'
home, he would tell us stories about his people.
He would describe the daily lives of the
children within their villages.
Also he described the games they would all play together.
We would marvel at all the great detail and
intricacies of his stories about children and the
young teenagers in the Pawnee village too.

Walking Bear and John would continue their talk
in Native Peoples language of the Pawnee.
They would laugh and carry on a happy conversation.
It made us feel better even though we have
seen the ugly side of our neighborhood.
To stay in this moment of clarity and happiness
made us want these times to never end.
Soon we saw these times end and
we had to try and live on.

Once we left his house, to go over and back into our own
houses, we would tell our parents about the wonderful
and exciting things we experienced being at his home.
They still showed their ignorance and
hatred toward Walking Bear.
We were all still in disbelief over the actions and words
of our parents who told us to treat everyone good and
how we should treat people as we are to be treated.

It seems our parents were hypocrites. They didn't
follow the core values they had set in us. It almost
made us want to be given up for adoption because
these monsters couldn't possibly be our parents.
We knew somewhere down the line karma would get our
parents back for being mean and hurtful toward Walking
Bear it was just a matter of time before their actions come
back to "bite them in the ass" as they would tell us about
evil doers in our cartoons we watched with our parents.

One of my parents told me, and other parents told my friends were going to prevent us from visiting our favorite Pawnee neighbor later on. To our chagrin they were adamant and very serious in keeping us from him. They began to follow us closely as we went outside to play.

A lot of times we would give them all the slip and try to go over there into Walking Bear's home. He would wave at us while we walked by his home and we would smile then wave back at him as we passed him by.

Still our parents on the way back to our home would ask, "Where did you go to today huh?" We would answer our parents saying, "We were around walking through the neighborhood." They didn't really believe us so they said, "Alright I guess we both believe you weren't over that Indian's home today."

Just like that a few days later, our parents went to
confront our friend the Pawnee neighbor. Their
prejudices and bigotry towards him was very apparent.
They began to tell him, "This is
America go away you Indian."
They said other really ignorant things.
Also saying, "Go get drunk Indian!"
Adding to this ignorant talk, "Why do you all still
live here anyway?" "You all should leave America!"
"We will never give you all your land throughout
North or South America or the Caribbean either."
This disgusted us very much hearing all the hatred,
bigotry and racism with intolerance mixed in.

Our friend had begun to see us without the notice
of our parents. He seemed a bit down from the
dark and sinister racism he felt from our very
ignorant parents and their bitter, resentful attitudes
toward him. He still appeared optimistic and
happy when talking to and being around us.

Even though he was highly upset at the treatment
he received from our parents. He still told more
stories about the Pawnee people, explaining about
the lives of the adults and elder of the village as well
talking of their daily trials and tribulations too.
We absorbed the stories as well. John was
always attentive to the stories as well.

Walking Bear had seemed even happier whenever John
would be by as he felt kinship there was another Native
Person of the Americas he could converse with.
John would smile as well too that a fellow Native
Person was who he could speak with.
Walking Bear said, "He had made the final
payment on his home and that in a day or
two he would have a surprise for us all."

We were in deep anticipation of what
he had to surprise us all.
He whispered something in John's ear. John nodded
and said something in Walking Bear's ear as well.

John Omar Larnell Adams

They hugged each other. Then Walking Bear
came over and told us we had to go home.

We left awaiting our surprise the next
time we were to visit Walking Bear.

One day we went by his home, he told us that
he was going to join his people. He explained
they were with "The Great Spirit".

We were saddened that he was leaving us forever.

Later he revealed to us, he was indeed a
ghost. We smiled because he in turn brought
happiness, joy and excitement to our lives.
He told John, "Rain Fire isn't time you joined us
with the Great Spirit with your wife Ruth?"
John said to him, "I will whenever she is ready
to take our final walk among the living."
We were surprised at John's answer to Walking Bear.
We asked John, "Are you a ghost to our friend?"
He laughed and said, "One day you will all
know the answer to that question."
Walking Bear had the sun shine on him. He began
walking in that light. More Native people came to greet
him. They waved at John. He waved back. Walking
Bear told us before going, "See you all it has been fun
watching you all, and spread the word of tolerance and
togetherness." He told John, "Rain Fire, you will join
us later." John nodded at him. He said something in
Pawnee to John who answered him back in Pawnee.

We cried as we said goodbye to Walking
Bear. He ascended into a line with the Native
Peoples spirits. The light disappeared.

John told us, "We have to keep living for
him and lead by his example friends."
We were still crying and nodded in
agreement to his statement.
John left soon after that to go back into Lexington,
Kentucky again. We miss him even to this day.

After all these years, I think of him daily. Pondering where in the afterlife he is and how he is getting along.

Despite the apprehension from our parents, we saw a great and wonderful person who became our dear friend. All this time I see one thing that is absolute:

There are many mysteries in the world, this life and universe. I had wondered what I saw: **Was it Really a Ghost**?

The answer is….. It really was.

The End

THEY WERE POSSESSED

Life in New York City is very fast. Sometimes you can stop in the middle of Times Square or other parts of the city, pause and look around, smile because you are in "The City that Never Sleeps!" My name is Tote Vision. I am a Native New Yorker.

Even though that is basically a bold or potentially racist notion, then I am not a member of any of the Native Peoples of the Americas tribes. So I think even though my family immigrated here to America and I was born here after my father grew up in this country as toddler brought here from England.

He married my mom a natural born U.S. citizen. Her family immigrated to America from Europe just like my father's family did. They met as teenagers in high school, dated, fell in love; then married and had me later on. My life was somewhat good or troublesome.

We had great times and my parents raised me well. My parents are Thomas and Sandy Vision.

I went through school and became an accountant, later I decided to ride out the bachelor life. My main friend at the accounting firm was Adriana Alexandra. She was great to me. Also we would compare stories of our Friday nights on Monday mornings to start the work week.

My daily life consisted of work and
adult play during the week.
I would go through files and help out clients
who needed their finances looked at.
While talking with clients about their financial
past, present and futures, I would discuss ways
for them to save money and spend money wisely
to keep up their spending habits responsible.

Also afterward I would go get lunch near
the office building where I worked.
Sometimes I would eat at a deli, getting a
Rueben sandwich with chips and a Pepsi.
Or I would go get a New York hotdog
from a hot dog vendor.
Other times I would go into a coffeehouse
and get a cappuccino with a Panini.

Once I got back into the office, the work continued.
Adriana would ask me, "What was good to eat for
lunch?" Just when soon as her lunchtime came up. I
gave her some of the places that I went to for lunch.
She told me, "Thanks Tote good sir." Just like
that I would smile at her and tell her, "Your
welcome beautiful friend of mine."

This would go on through the week
and soon Friday came up.

Adriana asked me, if I wanted to go out drinking
this Friday night which I accepted.

So after work we had left to go over at our bank
which we shared as our banking establishment.
Just as soon we both got over to there we checked our
accounts which had our direct deposits already in our
accounts we took 300 dollars each out of our accounts
and we got a taxi to go out so we could be at a bar near
our houses we lived three blocks away from each other.

So went to a no name bar and began to polish
off beer and different liquors and liqueurs.
We felt a buzz a first. Also we talked about
work and how are clients seemed to be clueless
about how to spend their money.

We also talked about our sexual conquests.
It seemed we were both oblivious to our
promiscuity we had shared between us.
Then we laughed about it and continued
pounding out drinks.
We paid for them as they kept coming from
the bartender and she had a male bartender
and I had a female bartender.

The laughs and jeers of the week began to wind
down as me and Adriana began to feel even drunker
from this night of "knocking back a few".

We decided to call it night finished paying off the last
of our drinks, Adriana had hailed down with her left

hand a taxi. We both got in and used the last of our money to pay the cab fare home. She got out to her place. I walked her to the door and made sure she got in okay. I had told her that, "I would call her as the second my drunken ass in my home." She laughed and said, "Well get your drunk ass home then."

I laughed too and got back in the cab, just then as soon that the three blocks to my condo were up. We made it to my condo.

After making it home, still pretty drunk, I paid the cabbie and made my way into my condo's building.

I sort of struggled to get into the door.
Everything was blurry and in a drunken haze.

To this day I don't know how I made it into my door.
After walking to the elevator, I got on it and
pressed the button to the 4th floor.
The door closed and I went upstairs.

After reaching my destination of the 4th floor, I saw my neighbors a couple married for a year or two. They were the Check family. The two of them were named Origin and Sara Check. They were from Boston and they could have been from New York, I guess that maybe I should get to know my neighbors better.

Later on I would regret getting to know them better.

It seems my neighbors were really good people.

Origin was a stock broker for a national firm.
Sara was either a prosecuting or defense lawyer
for a big New York City firm as well.
They seemed to have it all. Later on, I would soon find
out they had twin kids in college a young adult male and
female. Their kids were named Sharon and Wonder.

As it turned out their young adult kids would stop by in
the summer or winter for their breaks in University life.
They seemed like your average young adults with hopes
and dreams with underlying goals within those dreams.
For all the conversations I had with them, it
seemed Americas future was set if the country had
more bright and intelligible young people such as
these two as the future leaders of tomorrow.

Their parents would ask me, "How is
the bachelor's life treating me?"
I would answer, "Quite well and different women
on any given time at my beck and call."
They would also ask, "How my job is going?"
The answer I would give was, "It is fulfilling helping
people get financially literate and help them responsibly
apply their financial literacy into savings bonds and
other aspects of saving their money for later and
helping with the taxes that came along with it."

My neighbors were not too intrusive, just very warm
and welcoming if that was a saying to be said of them.

To this day I wonder if getting to know my
neighbors was a dark curse or "the writing
on the wall" about myself in particular.
They talked to me a little the next day on
Saturday morning when I decided to go out
for an unusual thing which was to jog.
They asked, "Trying to stay in shape for
the sex romps you have Tote?"

I told them, "No it is just I wanted to
try something different by jogging and
making myself a little bit healthier."
They nodded and said to me, "Good luck and watch out
for bicyclists and parked or moving cars and buses."
I laughed and said, "Thanks for the good
luck and enjoy your day neighbors."

So I went for my jog around the condo building
and up a few blocks. I saw Adriana coming home
from her usual jog on the weekend. We gave
pleasantries and said, "See you later good friend."

I continued jogging around the area. I felt
good even though the jog was getting taxing
in the winter day. As I continued into the last
leg of the jog the temperature got lower.
So I decided to go back to the condo and warm up a bit.

I began to hang out with my neighbors more
often. It seemed nothing was amiss yet.

One day they asked me when I came home from work
on a Wednesday night, "So Tote, good neighbor do you
want to go out for dinner and get drinks afterwards?"
I answered them, "Sure as long I don't
feel like a third wheel to you all."

They shook their heads and said to me, "No we would
like the company and we want to see where your head
is at and learn a little more about you that is all."
For that I smiled and said to them, "Well count me
in for dinner and drinks on Friday neighbors."

That Friday night had come up very quickly
and we went to a steakhouse and had dinner.
We discussed many subjects such as history,
family backgrounds, our childhoods, etc.
After a while and we were set as far the
feeling of being full off of food goes.

Soon we went to a bar some few blocks
away from the steakhouse.
We had order our first drinks a single pint of beer
for each of us. We sipped them very slowly.
As we chatted about the bar, the atmosphere of it and
the scenery of the bar, we all seemed to be on common
ground and could discuss just about anything.
I asked them, "What's it like to be
parents to young adults?"

They answered, "Like building a puzzle on
a Saturday afternoon, sure you know it has
to be done you just have to do it."

That analogy made me seem at ease and not like the odd
man out because of me having no children of my own.

So after having drinks, we left the bar and
caught a cab back to the condos.

I bid them adieu and they went to their
home and I went to mine.
I cut the lights on. Put my coat down and
began to wonder what else I could do with
my neighbors to seem interesting.
I changed into my pajamas and went to sleep.

John Omar Larnell Adams

Soon I asked Adriana if she would hang out with
me and my neighbors after work on our days off.

She agreed and like that she was off going to dinner
with the three of us and going to get drinks. It
seemed like a very fun situation at that time.
Little did I know that it was the beginning of a chain of
terrible events which would change or alter mine, Adriana
and the Check's lives forever in all of our lifetimes.

As Adriana hung out with me and the Check couple, we
all went to the same steakhouse and we went to the bar
from the first time I hung out with the Check family.
We all spoke of politics, gender issues,
masculinity, and femininity etc.

After going through all the beer, liquor and liqueur, we
all stumbled our way out of the bar. Completely wasted,
we all got in the same cab like we were sardines in a can.
Huddled together, we all laughed about on the
way. We started singing oldies songs to pass the
time between us and the condos we all lived in.

Adriana got to her place first. She paid the cabbie.
I walked her to the door and laughed about
being cramped together in the cab like that.
She couldn't stop laughing about it. She opened her door
to the building and made her way to the elevator. I waved
goodbye to her and made my way back to the cab.

The Check family and I began to sing more
oldies as we made our way to our condos.

We stopped and opened the door of the cab, paid
our cabbie and got to the front door of our condo
building. I unlocked the door and we all made
our way into the building and to the elevator.
As it came down I asked them, "That was
a great night wasn't it good people?"
They answered, "Yes it was, your friend Adriana
is quite the lady, and don't you think Tote?"
Then I answered, "Yes, she is a great woman and friend
too." I jokingly said, "Maybe I will marry her someday."
The Check family said out loud, "Tote
is in love, OOOOOH!"

We all laughed at the teasing, the elevator
came down and we got on it.
I pressed the 4th floor it went up to it. After the door
opened once it reached its destination, we got off
and made our ways to our respective homes. I waved
goodbye to them and said, "Good night great neighbors."
They told me back, "Good night dear Tote."

I shut my door, cut on the lights and began to put
my coat up in the closet in the front room. I took
my clothes off and changed into my pajamas. Then
clicked out the light to the living room, I then went
and flossed my teeth, brushed them and used a strong
mouthwash to kill the leftover germs in my mouth.

I felt refreshed and went to sleep.

Still as Adriana and I hung out with my neighbors, neither
of us ever suspected they were up to doing evil deeds.
We had continued the trek of going to different bars
so we had changed up our routine in bar hopping.
We talk about different subjects as usual like
history, ethics, law, business contracts; etc.
As usual we had got the best of each
others opinions on these topics.

I felt like the reversal of my life had taken place as if
I had reverted back to my childhood in class learning
something new from the life experience of the Check duo.
They were pretty good teachers and
students as were Adriana and I.

Once we got done drinking, we debated over the
city council's handling of New York City.
We didn't get into a heated discussion about
it, no not at all. We heard what each of us said
about our opinion and backed it up with facts
we read or heard from TV on our days off.

Once we all felt better about discussing local issues
it seemed our homes came upon us without fail.
Adriana got out first paid the cabbie and as
usual I walked her to her door and watched
her get in to walk toward the elevator.
I made my way back to the cab and talked some more
with the Check duo. As we made our way to our condos
as usual we felt elation the night was coming to an end.
We paid the cabbie and made our way to
the condo buildings front door.

242

Origin opened the door this time and we all made a B line
for the elevator and waited for it to come down as usual.
When it did we got on there, we giggled about
how slow the elevator was coming down.
Sara pressed the 4th floor button and we went up.

After reaching our destination, we left the elevator after
the door opened. We waved goodbye to each other and
made our way to the doors of our condos respectively.

I made my way inside and took off my coat
and changed clothes to pajamas. Did my
mouth cleaning ritual and went to sleep.

One day, my neighbors invited me by myself to
a special event held by them. It was at a specific
address in Manhattan. Little did I know the address
was at a condemned building on the Lower East
Side. The event that they held by what other things
I would later see them do was even more horrific
than the awful thing I saw committed this night.

After we got to the building, the Check duo
made their way inside and I did as well, they
told me to wait at the door they pointed at
for me to meet them at in 10 minutes.

Soon after 10 minutes passed, they told me,
"Go inside the door and wait for us Tote."
So I went inside, and heard Mozart's Don
Giovanni on a MP3 player with speakers.
I was taken aback because the room was dark
and the only light was the MP3 player.

I heard a female moaning slowly, almost sensually.
Just then, as I had quickly turned to the direction of
where I heard all this and to try and find the source of
the mock orgasm like moaning from this woman in the
background of this room. I had seen the lights come on.
It was a sparse light it seemed the woman being held in
place by something which seemed to be hanging from
the ceiling of this dimly lit room was just in the moment.
I could smell her arousal as her snatch gave a distinct
smell as she was very horny from what I could smell.

Just like that a costumed duo came through the door in
masks and some sort of cult like robes with sandals on.
They said to me in a hurried voice, "Move God Dammit!"
I was then brushed aside.

The woman who had been moaning was fully seen now.
She was completely naked, as I tried to get my bearings
my neighbors swung into action with this woman.
As the music kept on playing, I saw my neighbor
Origin take his dong and penetrate this woman
from behind in her asshole. His wife Sara
used a strap on to penetrate her vagina.

As they took turns violating this woman. I stood
there with my mouth open as they continually
thrust fast and hard inside this woman. They
began punching her and Sara started using a box
cutter on this woman cutting her up a bit.
They grabbed iodine and rubbing alcohol on her cuts.
She writhed sexually and moaned loudly from this
sexual deviance. It seemed she liked pain and pleasure.

Sara was very wet from this act of being the penetrator
to this bound woman. I could smell both of their
snatches scent as this sick double penetration and
S&M with bondage depravity continued.

Soon both Sara and the woman climaxed,
squirting and coming everywhere.
Origin had an orgasm inside this woman's asshole.

After they finished they let the woman down from her
bound arms to the ceiling. My neighbors changed back
into their clothes, we caught a cab and went home.

After having had I started seeing all these
awful events this night, my neighbors walked
me home. They then told me to relax.
I was still mortified from what I had seen by
neighbors, the hedonism, depravity, sadism and
masochism which decried a certain evil even
I hadn't seen before especially in them.

It was almost too much to take in from just this
night which also started the end of our friendship
by these and later actions done by the Check duo.

Still kind of distraught from all these actions I had
seen, my thoughts were coming together slowly.
I asked the two of them, "So how long have you two
been doing this kind of sexual deviance and assault,
lastly mending of those you defile in a sense?"

The two of them answered, "Since we left
college in Boston in the 1970's."
Taken aback from all this information I told
them, "So it's been going on over 20 years."
They answered me, "Yes Tote good man it has been over
20 years." They added by asking, "Why don't you join in
our fun it's enjoyable and it gives you an adjusted rush?"

I told them, "I can't get involved with that kind
of thing it will make me an even worse kind of

bachelor, the kind of man I feel couldn't capable
of this kind of perverse, depraved kind of fun."

The Check duo said to me, "Sucks
to be you Tote good man!"
With that the cab stopped in front of our condo's building
and we got out, Sara opened the door and we stepped in.

After we got inside the building I pressed
the button to the elevator.
As it came down sweat came down my face in attempt
to cool me off from the event I had seen that night.
The elevator came down and we all got
on it I pressed the 4th floor button.

The door closed and we made it past the other floors,
soon the 4th floor had arrived. We got off the elevator,
the Check family duo waved goodbye to me as we parted
from each other. I had waved back at them. Then I
unlocked my door, made my way as I did the Check
family duo made their way into their condo's door.

I had made my way inside my condo, switched on
the living room light, took my coat off made my way
into my room, cut on its light; put my pajamas on,
brushed, flossed and used mouthwash on my teeth.
Cut out all the lights and went to sleep in my bed.

More and more, I would hang out with my
neighbors. Even more sinister things went on.

Like demonic rituals, demonic possession, animal
sacrifice; people tortured, people beaten, people
raped and people sodomized by both of them.

They asked me, "How about you try some of
this stuff out with us Tote our good man."
I nervously said to them, "This is a bit too kinky
and disturbing for my taste good neighbors."
They told me then, "It's alright you're
just a pussy is all Tote good man."
They laughed at their sentiment and we
went about hanging out still in condemned
buildings around Manhattan.
The work week seemed not to come on fast enough.

As I worked every day during the work week, my
days seemed shorter as the work load increased and
decreased during the beginning and end of the week.
I talked to clients still about their
financial futures, past and present.
My favorite clients seemed to be inclined to talk
with me about their daily lives which put me at ease
from the weekends of seeing the Check family duo
engaging in their precarious activities with women
and Sara with the men they also strung up to the
ceiling of those condemned buildings basements.

Then Friday would come and the Check family
duo even would come get me to go over into

the other parts of Manhattan to watch them
engage in their depravity, torture, and occult
activity preoccupation lastly sexual deviance.

This stuff even happened on Saturday nights as well.
It troubled me because I could have called one of
my ladies and went to go "bang the shit" out of her
than watch other people just defile these women.

Monday, had come up soon enough.

At work, I look disheveled and distraught by these odd happenings I was witnessing on a daily basis. I told Adriana, who laughed because of the pedigree and clean cut, sophisticated goodness she saw of my neighbors the times she hung out with us those times.

I told her, "It is starting to wear on me, almost desensitizing me to the horrible acts I see with them on given weekends." Then I added, "They make the rapists, sadists and depraved people on crime dramas, seem like Mr. Rogers Adriana." She laughed even harder and said to me, "No way I don't believe they would do something like that Tote." She added, "No they can't do or wouldn't do bad things like that."

I tried to still convince her my neighbors were horrible and deprave individuals. She shook her head and said to me, "I will believe you if they invite me to one of these events you have described to me Tote good friend of mine." I felt beside myself as trying to convince her that my neighbors aren't who she thinks they are.

So I mentioned to the Check family duo that Adriana wanted to be a special guest like me to one of their special events where they either sodomize, rape or physically assault men and women.

The two of them said to me, "We will personally invite that chick you're in love with Tote good man."

My thoughts seemed clouded by their casual answer to me.

Friday crept up on us just like it always did.

So Adriana was personally invited to by my
neighbors' special event. She didn't know and
I didn't know what was in store for us at the
location we were assigned to go over to.

The Check family duo told the two of us to
wait at the door. I answered them, "You're
right we will be here waiting for you."

Adriana was confused as to what was happening. She
asked me, "What's up Tote?" Then she added, "I wonder
just what am I about to see in this old ass building and
why the fact is it that you are sweating so much?'

I wanted to tell her or warn her about the
perverted and depraved things she would see.
So I told her, "You're in for an either good or
off the wall experience tonight Adriana."
She nodded as we were inclined to go through the
door leading to whatever sick, perverted and depraved
individual we would see get basically violated tonight.

As we got into the room we saw a light flickering
on and off on two people a tall muscular
man and a voluptuous woman both bound
to the ceiling with their arms tied to it.
After the light shone on them the music played
it was Don Giovanni by Mozart. I felt that opera
music made this even more uncomfortable to view.
Adriana was awestruck by the tall, naked muscular
man bound to the ceiling and I was taken aback by
the beautiful woman naked and completely curvy.

As we marveled at the gorgeous specimens in front of us, Origin and Sara made their way past us and slightly pushing us saying, "Out of the way fuckers!"

As they made their way to the beautiful people awaiting to be violated, I could smell both Adriana and Sara's wet snatches as they had pure lust for the naked and muscular man. Origin seemed to have a huge bulge in his pants for the curvy and gorgeous woman. Sara had a strap on attached to her crotch again. The two of them taking their fake phallic and real penis and entered both separately, Origin inside the woman in both her snatch and asshole. Thrusting and pumping her madly, hard and fast. Sara had begun to enter the man's asshole and what they call pegging now she violated that man. Both the woman and the man moaned loudly and said, "Fuck me harder god dammit!" The Check family duo went faster and harder with rhythmic pumps. Also they had beat up and cut the man and woman separately. While cleaning there wounds as well.

After climaxing Sara squirted and her female ejaculate ran down her legs. The strap on was still on her crotch area. Origin climaxed inside the curvy and beautiful woman's cookie and in her asshole separately. That woman had her leg shake as she orgasm med and squirted as she came while Origin came inside her.

Adriana was intensely wet from this sexual deviance. I was still hard from seeing this woman get violated. I felt a sense of oddness from all this. Sara and Origin changed back into their clothes. Untied the

man and woman. Then those two, me and Adriana
caught a cab and went back to our condos.

After the event, Adriana kept quiet around me. She
slipped and stuck a post it to my desk calendar. It said,
"I might need to start therapy from that event!"
I told her, "See I didn't lie to you about them."
She nodded, and we both looked like we needed sleep.
The times of hanging out with them was becoming more
than we could handle even by our weirdness scale.

Adriana and I had tried to keep up appearances
despite all the twisted and somewhat off
putting depravity and perversion we saw each
weekend with the Check family duo.

I thought the last time was the end of me seeing the
Check family duo ravage people was over. How wrong
I was. I had received a call from the Check family duo
to experience one more instance of their depravity.

I accepted and told them, "My good people
let this be the very last time please?"
They agreed and said to me, "Don't worry, Tote my
good man this will be a treat for you and us."

So that Friday came upon me very soon.

My neighbors invited me to another event. What
I saw happen next shocked and appalled me.

As I waited for them by the door as usual, they
told me, "Something special is happening to
our guest this night Tote good man."
I wondered what they meant by that.
My curiosity was peaked by their notion for this night as
it seemed like their usual time of doing the awful deeds
they would do to any given man or woman or both.
As I made my way into this new old condemned
building's special room, the special guest for
tonight would rock me to my core.

As I walked into the room, I saw a naked woman
and who it was as the light shone on this mystery
woman still sends hard and cold chills up my spine.
The woman was Adriana. I asked the Check
family duo about this happening, "Why
is Adriana here Origin and Sara?"
They answered me chillingly saying, "We just
thought how fun it would be to have our way with
her. They added, "So we drugged her a bit."

My stomach had severe approaching nausea
from this development. The whole act of seeing
Adriana all disoriented and completely high
"off her ass" startled and appalled me.

The music played again it was Tchaikovsky's Piano
Concerto No.1, I was taken aback from the emotional

depth of the classical piece. It was a prelude and
amalgamation of every emotion I would feel this night.

The Check family killed a chicken and spread
its blood on Adriana's big breasted chest. They
said something which either resembled Wiccan
incantation or Voodoo incantation.
Soon it seemed a sensual and sexual
spirit implanted itself in Adriana.
She spoke in an unfamiliar tongue
to the Check family duo.

The two of them went up to Adriana, Possessed by
whatever demon, her nipples perked up, very aroused
and wet she was as then Sara was and Origin was very
hard from this. The strap on Sara was wearing dangled
and was protruding. She entered Adriana in the asshole.
While Origin entered her in her pussy. They began
banging the living shit out of her. She moaned in ecstasy,
Sara was creaming in her pants and I could smell it.

Origin was making weird animal noises as he
was "going in" with Adriana screwing her like
an experienced man goes in on a virgin.
They hit her and cut her a bit. Adriana's eyes rolled
in the back of her head. She let out more moans. I
heard something in the background like a machine.
I turned it was a camera filming this. I realized that
I had heard that noise every time I was here.
They had been recording every person they violated
in each place. After the two of the Check family
duo climaxed, Adriana shook hard and came

hard squirting and her leg, then body didn't stop
shaking. Origin came in her. Sara squirted again
and it dripped into the sandals she wore.
Everyone came to their senses. The Check
family duo untied her. I put her clothes back
on her then we all went caught a cab.
I took Adriana to her place and took her inside and
laid her in the bed she owned and left for my condo.

After the traumatic experience done to Adriana,
I felt guilt for inviting her to any of the events.
Also I felt despair and sorrow from seeing her
twisted and disturbed face during and after the
ordeal. What it must have done to her psyche.

I couldn't begin to rationalize anything which
would bring her back from that night. That
night made me hate the Check's period.
They took someone I cherished and loved deeply
and distorted her beyond repair mentally and
physically with their kinks in fetishes.

The more I tried to console her she seemed
withdrawn and scared completely, I thought it
would take a long time to get her back to normal.

I kept trying to talk to her. She felt withdrawn
and emotionally dead inside.

It took time to reconcile her psyche. My patience with
ineptitude to help her in the first place had me reeling.

So onto the next phase of this story.......

The NYPD, had came to our workplace and told
me to come with them because they needed answers
to questions all which needed to be answered.
They had been having a swift criminal investigation
looking at the lives of my neighbors. As to which lead to a
crackdown of bad or deviant behavior to its extreme detail.

They asked me about my neighbors, the Check family.
I gave them just the things I know about them. Also
I told them we had all went out to go drinking on
some Fridays and ate at different restaurants as well.

The police seemed happy that they got more
information out of me than anyone else.
I felt awful snitching on the Check family duo. The
fact of the matter is they had hurt and traumatized
someone I loved and cherished more than anyone else.

They were my friends and seeing the women and men
they did awful things to in the name of being kinky and
fetishes made unnerved and I had hit my breaking point
seeing Adriana bound to a ceiling, drugged, beaten, cut,
sodomized and double penetrated hard, fast and rough.

So I decided that my friends needed to be locked away
a while and be around either equally sick or even more
sick individuals in separate prisons who would do either
the same to the two of them like they did to others
or even worst things to them in their prison cells.

My neighbors were later arrested. The police found all kinds of troubling things in their possession.

Candles, whips, chains, knives, dildoes, pocket vaginas etc. A pervert, or sadist or depraved and sexually deviant people owned kind of stuff. My other neighbors just said, "Oh Shit they are some kinky motherfuckers and twisted too!"

I just nodded with them. Some asked me, "Didn't you go with them to watch their depravity, sadism, masochism and perversion Tote; in those condemned buildings in other parts of Manhattan?"

I had answered them honestly with a statement that still leaves me wondering where I or both of them went wrong, "Yes they were my friends and I saw firsthand what the two of them were capable of my neighbor."

My other neighbor nodded and said, "You might be just as sick then the two of them because you enjoyed watching the shit."

To his revelation I answered him, "You know maybe you're right about that man."
I couldn't shrug off that I was just as bad as the Check family duo for watching with awe and not trying to put a stop to their twisted, depraved, sadistic and perverted fun. He said to me what I realized once I was in that condemned building the first time I walked through the door of that basement room

and watch the kinky and weird fetish my neighbors were doing to this bound yet beautiful, vulnerable and sexually deviant woman I saw that first night that I had experienced the evil of my neighbors.

After getting her treated psychologically, Adriana slowly but surely got back to normal. We developed a serious relationship with each other. We started a family too. Before our children became toddlers or even when they slept, sometimes we would talk about the good old days.

Even us sitting and talking about the troubling times with my neighbors, Adriana found talking about it was being very cathartic to her.
These things cross my mind after we're finishing talking and Adriana finally goes to sleep:

When thinking of my neighbors, they both seemed normal, after they did what those horrible, evil things to Adriana and others; the two of them had done and after they were apprehended. It seemed ***They Were Possessed.***

The End

Thanks for reading!

Printed in the United States
By Bookmasters